Wrinkleskin Stories

OrangeBooks Publication

1st Floor, Rajhans Arcade, Mall Road, Kohka, Bhilai, Chhattisgarh 490020

Website: **www.orangebooks.in**

© Copyright, 2024, Author

All rights reserved. No part of this book may be reproduced, stored in a retrieval system, or transmitted, in any form by any means, electronic, mechanical, magnetic, optical, chemical, manual, photocopying, recording or otherwise, without the prior written consent of its writer.

First Edition, 2024

ISBN: 978-93-6554-430-5

Wrinkleskin Stories

Short Stories Etched by Time, Celebrating the Wisdom and Warmth of Our Elders

ASHWIN KUMAR IYER

OrangeBooks Publication
www.orangebooks.in

To all the elders, whose wisdom, memories, and quiet sacrifices have shaped us. This book is a tribute to the enduring light you cast on our lives, guiding us through the stories you leave behind.

Preface

In an era marked by rapid change and fleeting connections, I often find myself reflecting on the beauty of lives lived fully, shaped by tradition, love, and the wisdom of time. As I wrote these stories, I was drawn to the voices of our elders, their journeys interwoven with the vibrant culture of India. Each of these tales is a tribute to the quiet resilience and enduring strength of our senior generations—those who carry not only their own memories but also the weight of our collective history.

In *Wrinkleskin Stories*, I have sought to capture moments that resonate with the universality of aging, yet remain deeply rooted in the unique customs, values, and emotions of South Indian life. These stories explore more than nostalgia; they are reflections on family, community, and the inevitable passage of time. From the laughter shared beneath the village banyan tree to the silent joys and sorrows found in a forgotten letter, each narrative is imbued with memories that shape and sustain us.

As you journey through these pages, I hope you will see our elders not only as individuals from a bygone era but as a living bridge to our roots. May this collection serve as a reminder of the invaluable wisdom that often goes unspoken and the lives that, though perhaps softened by age, remain filled with spirit and grace.

Thank you for taking the time to join me in honouring these stories. They are close to my heart, and I hope they bring you moments of warmth, understanding, and perhaps a glimpse of your own history and heritage.

With gratitude,

Ashwin Kumar Iyer

Stories And Synopses

The Last Train to Thiruvananthapuram
Seventy-year-old Narayan Pillai has always longed to visit his childhood home in Thiruvananthapuram. His children are too busy to accompany him, but a chance encounter with a young IT Professional spark an unexpected friendship. Together, they embark on the journey, rekindling memories and finding healing in the simple acts of kindness along the way.

Mangoes for Radhamma
Every summer, Radhamma waits eagerly for her grandchildren to visit her village home and enjoy the mangoes from her beloved trees. But as the years pass, visits grow sparse. When a young neighbour realizes how much Radhamma misses her family, he devises a plan to bring her the joy she deserves, reminding the village of the value of companionship and family bonds.

The Temple Keeper's Secret
Krishnamurthy, the oldest caretaker of an old temple, is entrusted with a secret that has been passed down through generations. As developers plan to turn the area into a shopping complex, Krishnamurthy faces a choice: share the secret and save the temple or remain silent. His story uncovers the delicate balance between tradition and

progress, and the wisdom elders bring in preserving culture.

A Saree for Amma

In a small coastal village near Cuddalore, Lakshmi misses her late mother deeply. She decides to buy herself a saree just like the ones her mother wore, hoping it will help her feel closer to her memory. But when her own daughter sees Lakshmi wearing it, she gains a new perspective on her mother's life, rekindling her desire to care for her as her mother once did.

The Scooter Ride

Ramanujam, once a daring motorbike rider in his youth, now feels forgotten as he struggles to move around the bustling city of Bengaluru. One day, his granddaughter offers to take him on a scooter ride around town. The day out rekindles his zest for life, and the experience brings both generations closer, as they share stories and laughter across the city's landscape.

The Banyan Tree Meetings

Under a sprawling banyan tree in a Tamil Nadu village, a group of elderly men meet daily to discuss life, share memories, and exchange advice. When a young government official tries to remove the tree to build a road, the group bands together, reminding the community of the value these elders bring, both in wisdom and as living history keepers of the village.

Songs for Savithri

Once a Carnatic singer, Savithri Amma has grown quiet in her old age. Her family no longer has time to listen to her sing. When a young music student moves in next door, he hears her humming and encourages her to sing once more. Their friendship brings her voice back to life, rekindling her spirit and showing her family the importance of cherishing her talents.

The Forgotten Dance

Gowri, a retired schoolteacher from Madurai, once loved Bharatanatyam and gave up her dreams for family life. Her old friends visit, coaxing her into performing for the neighbourhood children. The event breathes new life into her and sparks a newfound admiration for her among the younger generation, who learn about the sacrifices made by their elders.

Letters from the Past

Sixty-eight-year-old Krishna finds a stack of old love letters he wrote to his wife in his youth. Reading through them, he reflects on the years gone by and the deep bond they shared. His children, seeing the letters, begin to understand the romance and struggles of their parents' lives, learning to appreciate the enduring love that sustained their family.

The Tea Seller's Wisdom

Moideen, a former tea seller at a busy railway station in Kerala, now spends his days at home, feeling forgotten. When his grandson starts a local blog, he interviews

Moideen about his days at the station. Through his stories of travellers and kindness, Moideen's wisdom resonates with the community, highlighting the importance of listening to and valuing the elderly in modern life.

INDEX

Last Train To Thiruvananthapuram 1

Mangoes For Radhamma 11

The Temple Keeper's Secret 29

A Saree For Amma 47

The Scooter Ride 61

The Banyan Tree Meetings 79

Songs For Savithri 96

The Forgotten Dance 114

Letters From The Past 130

The Tea Seller's Wisdom 147

Afterword 165

Last Train To Thiruvananthapuram

Narayan Pillai, a man of seventy years, sat by the balcony window, watching life unfurl on the streets below his modest apartment. The sounds of distant traffic, the bells from the temple, and the call of vendors were his constants now, woven seamlessly into his day. Yet in his heart, a different music played—a melody of memories, of laughter and running barefoot across sun- warmed fields, of rivers and temples and age-old banyan trees. He had not returned to his childhood home in Thiruvananthapuram for decades. "I'll go next month," he'd say to his wife, back when he still had her by his side. And now, with time a gentle but persistent reminder, he felt the tug again, more potent than ever.

But his children—Vishwanath and Leela—were far too busy for such sentimental excursions. "Appa, it's a long journey for you to make alone," they'd say with concern, though he knew they were thinking more of their schedules than his fragility. They lived busy lives in Mumbai and Bangalore, worlds away from the languid pace of Thiruvananthapuram. For them, time was a matter of business calls, deadlines, and quick visits over weekends, leaving little room for their father's yearning.

Yet the urge persisted, gnawing gently, like the whisper of the breeze through the palms that had once shaded his home. And so, on a quiet Monday morning, he took out an old leather bag, dusted it, and placed it by his chair— a reminder to himself that he would, indeed, go. When and how were mysteries still unfurling, but his heart had decided.

It was around this time that he met Arjun. Arjun was a young IT professional, fresh-faced, with an eagerness that the years had not yet weathered. Narayan Pillai spotted him first at the tea stall by the corner, trying to order his masala chai in broken Tamil. Narayan couldn't help but chuckle at his struggle.

"Oh, young man," he called out, "that's not how you order tea here! Just say 'stronga oru tea kudunga'— strong tea, please."

Arjun grinned sheepishly. "Thank you, sir," he said, with a deference that made Narayan warm to him immediately. They fell into an easy conversation, as naturally as the tea simmered on the stall owner's stove. Arjun was new to the city, having transferred from Bangalore for a short project stint. Alone and homesick, he found in Narayan an unexpected anchor—a familiar face in a sea of strangers.

Over the next few days, Narayan and Arjun met regularly. They would chat about everything under the sun— Arjun's work, his family in Kerala, the quirks of life in Chennai. In his quiet way, Narayan would share stories of his childhood, his schooling, and the mischief he and his brothers used to get into.

One afternoon, as the sun began to dip, casting an amber hue over the streets, Arjun noticed a distant look in Narayan's eyes.

"You're thinking of somewhere far away, aren't you, sir?" he asked gently.

Narayan nodded, his gaze lost in some distant past. "Thiruvananthapuram," he said, the name like a soft sigh. "It's where I grew up. I've always wanted to go back...one last time."

There was a pause as Arjun considered this. "Why don't you, sir?" he asked simply. "What holds you back?"

Narayan's laugh was soft, almost resigned. "Oh, my children say it's too much for an old man like me. They mean well, of course, but..." he shrugged, as if dismissing a persistent fly.

Arjun's face brightened. "Then let me come with you, sir! I have a few days off next week, and I've never really seen Thiruvananthapuram. It would be an honour to travel with you."

Narayan was taken aback. Here was a young man, barely half his age, with a thousand things to do, offering to accompany an old stranger on what seemed to others a trivial pilgrimage. "Are you sure?" he asked, searching Arjun's face, almost afraid that the young man would take back his offer in the next breath.

Arjun smiled, his eyes earnest. "Yes, sir. I'd like to go. It will be an adventure."

And so it was settled. The following week, Narayan Pillai and Arjun boarded the train to Thiruvananthapuram together.

The train journey was long, but for Narayan, it passed in the blink of an eye. He took in the sights along the way— paddy fields stretching like green carpets, rivers flowing lazily, and villages where children ran barefoot after goats. Arjun sat beside him, listening intently as Narayan recounted tales of his youth with a twinkle in his eye.

"Ah, those were simpler times," Narayan mused, watching a group of women washing clothes by a riverbank as the train passed. "We didn't have much, but life felt full—of laughter, of little joys. Even a piece of jaggery felt like a feast."

Arjun listened, a little awestruck by the details, the way Narayan remembered even the scents and sounds. In his stories, Arjun sensed the true Thiruvananthapuram, not just a place but a world filled with vibrant characters and timeless values.

They ate from little packets of banana chips and rice wrapped in banana leaves, and Narayan shared tips on how to tell a good chip from a mediocre one. Arjun was fascinated by the small things—the way Narayan would wipe his fingers on a handkerchief before taking a sip of water, the quiet reverence he had for the simplest of foods, and the care he took with each morsel.

As they neared Thiruvananthapuram, the evening sun bathed the landscape in golden light, and Narayan grew quiet, his eyes fixed on the scenery that was slowly but surely becoming familiar. For Arjun, it was a glimpse into another world—a gentler world, where time moved at a different rhythm.

Finally, as the train rolled into the Thiruvananthapuram station, Narayan felt his heart leap. He could hardly believe he was here. All the years he had dreamed of this moment, and now it was real, within his reach.

Arjun smiled at him, sensing his joy. "Welcome home, sir," he said simply, and in that moment, Narayan felt a lump in his throat. This young man, a stranger only days ago, had become a friend—a bridge to a past he had feared lost.

And as they stepped off the train together, Narayan knew that this journey was only the beginning.

The air of Thiruvananthapuram was thick with the scent of jasmine and sandalwood, laced with the faint, comforting aroma of burning incense drifting from the nearby temples. Narayan Pillai took it all in, feeling both foreign and familiar in a place that was once his world. The old man moved carefully, his gaze tracing the crumbling yet steadfast buildings, the narrow streets that wound around corners, the little shops that hadn't changed much over the years.

"Sir, where shall we go first?" Arjun asked, keeping a respectful distance. He had grown fond of Narayan in their short time together, fascinated by the way the older man treated life with quiet reverence.

Narayan thought for a moment, a smile spreading across his face. "There's a small temple by the river, tucked away from the bustle of the main road," he said softly. "My mother would take me there every Friday. I haven't seen it since I was a boy."

They walked through the winding streets, Arjun helping Narayan navigate the uneven ground. Children played marbles in the street, their laughter filling the air. A vendor called out, selling fresh coconut water, and a pair of cows lazed by a tea stall. As they approached the river, the sight of the temple came into view—a small, humble shrine, nestled among trees that seemed to guard it with a quiet dignity.

Narayan's steps slowed, his face filled with wonder. Time had softened the temple's colours, faded the paint, but it still stood, solid and serene. The memories of his mother's hand guiding him up the stone steps flooded his mind, warm and clear.

"I was barely five when I first came here," he murmured. "The priest would give me a handful of rice and a sweet. For me, it was a feast." He chuckled softly, lost in the memory.

Arjun watched him with respect, sensing the depth of emotion in his companion's gaze. "Sir, would you like to go inside?" he asked.

Narayan nodded, and they entered together. Inside, the temple was quiet, the air thick with incense. A young priest greeted them, his eyes brightening at the sight of Narayan's reverence.

They stood there for a while, Narayan's eyes closed in silent prayer. When he opened them, he looked over at Arjun and smiled. "Thank you," he said quietly. "I think my mother would be glad to see me here."

After leaving the temple, they strolled through the nearby market, where stalls bustled with activity, selling everything from fresh bananas to intricately woven baskets. Narayan bought a few sweets wrapped in banana leaves, the kind he remembered from his youth. Arjun took one, marvelling at the simplicity and flavour.

As the day wore on, Narayan guided Arjun to other places he remembered. The corner where he'd spent his allowance on peanuts, the riverside where he'd once tried—and failed—to fish with his friends, the old school building that still stood, a little faded but proud. Each place carried a memory, and with each step, Narayan seemed to regain a piece of himself that he had thought lost to time.

It was at the edge of the riverbank that Narayan felt the day's emotions catch up to him. He sat down on a stone, watching the water flow by, the same river that had been his friend and companion as a boy.

"Arjun," he began slowly, his voice thick with emotion, "I thought coming here would make me sad, that I'd only see the ghosts of things gone by. But you know, it doesn't feel like that at all. Instead, it feels… whole. Like I can finally see my life as it was and as it is now, all woven together."

Arjun nodded, moved by the old man's quiet revelation. "It sounds like you're at peace, sir," he said softly.

"Yes," Narayan replied. "Yes, I think I am. For so long, I was worried about everything I'd left behind, as if I had abandoned my memories, my childhood. But now I see that they were always with me, part of me." He smiled, looking at Arjun. "And I wouldn't have come to realize this if it weren't for you."

They spent the rest of the evening wandering the streets of Thiruvananthapuram. Arjun absorbed every detail, taking in the spirit of the city through Narayan's eyes. To him, this trip was more than an excursion; it was a glimpse into a life both deeply rooted and profoundly meaningful.

When night fell, they returned to a small guesthouse Arjun had booked for them, its balcony overlooking the softly lit streets. As they sat under the starlit sky, Narayan grew reflective again.

"Arjun," he said, his voice barely above a whisper, "it's strange, isn't it? This journey, this place, it has reminded me of so much—but it has also shown me something new." He paused, searching for the right words. "You've given me something my children could not… a chance to remember and to share, without rush or restraint."

Arjun looked at him with a mixture of respect and gratitude. "Sir, I think you've given me more than I've given you. I came here to help you, but I feel I've learned more about myself, about life. And… thank you for letting me be part of your journey."

Narayan patted his shoulder. "Sometimes, Arjun, in life, we are given people who help us see things we would otherwise miss. You were that person for me."

The next morning, they packed their things, ready to catch the train back to Chennai. As they boarded, Narayan felt a contentment settle over him, warm and satisfying. He had come to Thiruvananthapuram looking for something he hadn't been able to name—and he'd found it, not in the streets or buildings, but in the peace that came from knowing his memories and his present life were not so far apart after all.

As the train chugged along, he looked over at Arjun, who had fallen asleep against the window, his face calm. Narayan smiled, feeling a surge of affection for the young man who had, in his quiet way, become part of his own story.

For the rest of the journey, Narayan gazed out the window, his mind quiet. The fields, rivers, and trees passed by, blurring like the chapters of his life—a life now fully seen, understood, and embraced.

And when they finally returned to Chennai, Narayan Pillai stepped off the train, not as the man who had left, but as one who had found something precious—something as timeless as the land of Thiruvananthapuram itself.

Mangoes For Radhamma

On the outskirts of Salem, under the searing blue sky and amidst the fields that stretched into undulating hills, Radhamma sat on her woven cot, squinting into the horizon. She was waiting, as she did each summer, for her grandchildren to arrive. Her old fingers traced invisible patterns on the cot's worn surface, her mind lost in the memory of young feet scampering around her courtyard, eager hands reaching out to pluck mangoes, and a din of laughter filling her home.

Radhamma was nearing eighty now, though she didn't care to count her years. They had seemed to accumulate quietly, like dust on the mango trees she loved so dearly. Each year, those trees yielded a bounty of fruit, plump and golden, their fragrance thickening the air. The trees had been a constant in her life, silent companions that stood witness to her journey as a wife, a mother, and now, a grandmother. She tended to them with the same devotion, mindful of their watering and pruning, and in return, they offered their fruit generously. The mangoes—her mangoes—were the pride of the village, and Radhamma took pleasure in sharing them with her kin.

But as the years passed, her house had grown quieter. Once, the arrival of summer meant a house full of children, running, laughing, and filling the air with stories from the city. Her grandchildren had been the heartbeats of her home, their laughter echoing in her ears even after they had left. But now, the visits had grown sparse. Her son and daughter-in-law, absorbed in their work, rarely made time for the village, and the children—well, they were grown now, with lives that seemed too busy for an old woman and her mangoes.

Yet, Radhamma's hope remained undimmed. Every year, when the mango trees were laden with fruit, she would arrange the courtyard with fresh rangoli, sweep the house till it was spotless, and prepare the beds for the children. She would sit on her cot, her eyes fixed on the dusty road that led to her house, waiting for a sight of them, for the burst of laughter that would sweep through her house once more.

This year was no different. The first wave of mangoes had ripened, their sweet fragrance filling the courtyard, promising an abundant harvest. Radhamma had already started setting aside the ripest ones, arranging them in bamboo baskets. Each morning, she rose with renewed hope, preparing the house and cooking the children's favourite dishes. "They will come," she assured herself, though a little voice inside whispered that they might not.

The village people knew of Radhamma's waiting, and sometimes, they would come to sit with her, sharing news of their children, bringing her the comfort of companionship. But none of them understood the ache that gnawed at her heart, the silent yearning for her family.

One afternoon, as she sat by her door, she noticed a boy from the neighbourhood walking past. His name was

Ravi, a curious little fellow with a wide grin and bright eyes, always asking questions and running errands for the villagers. Radhamma had watched him grow from a scrawny child into a tall, lanky lad who seemed to take an interest in everything around him. He was always up to something, whether it was helping the village carpenter or sneaking into the fields for a taste of unripe tamarind.

Ravi noticed her watching him and grinned. "Amma, waiting for someone?" he asked with that easy familiarity, plopping himself down beside her.

Radhamma smiled, a little embarrassed. "Yes, my grandchildren. They promised to come this year."

Ravi looked at the mangoes piled in her courtyard and raised an eyebrow. "They must be lucky, Amma. These mangoes look delicious. I wish I could eat them all."

Radhamma chuckled. "If they don't come soon, you might just get the chance."

The boy looked at her thoughtfully, and for a moment, Radhamma felt as if he understood her. "I'm sure they'll come, Amma," he said, though there was a hint of doubt in his voice. "Why wouldn't they? You make the best mango pickles in the whole village!"

Radhamma laughed, but her laughter was tinged with sadness. She knew the boy was trying to cheer her up, and she appreciated his kindness. Yet, as the days passed, her heart grew heavier, the weight of waiting pressing down on her.

One evening, Ravi, who had been watching her closely all summer, came up with an idea. He had always been fond of Radhamma and had spent many afternoons sitting with her, listening to her stories of the old days, marvelling at her memory and wisdom. To him, she was like the grandmother he never had, and he couldn't bear to see her so lonely.

Ravi waited until dusk, when the air was cool and the village quiet. He found his friend Murugan, who lived down the street, and whispered his plan. Murugan listened, nodding enthusiastically. "That's a great idea,

Ravi! She'll be thrilled!" he said, clapping his friend on the back.

The boys spent the next few days gathering their friends, whispering in secret, and making plans. They knew Radhamma's grandchildren wouldn't be coming this year; word had spread that her family was too busy in the city. But that didn't mean she had to be alone. Ravi and the other children of the village decided to fill her courtyard with laughter and chatter, to make her mango season as joyful as it used to be.

On a bright Saturday morning, Ravi led a small procession of children to Radhamma's house. They were armed with baskets, wide smiles, and a mischievous glint in their eyes. As they approached her house, Ravi called out, "Amma! Look who's here!"

Radhamma, who had been sweeping the courtyard, looked up, startled. Her eyes widened as she saw the children streaming into her house, filling it with noise and energy. They laughed, they called her name, and before she could say anything, they had scattered into the courtyard, picking up the ripe mangoes and passing them around.

For a moment, Radhamma just stood there, bewildered. But then, a smile crept onto her face, a smile that grew wider as the children peeled the mangoes, their sticky fingers and eager faces a sight she hadn't seen in years. Ravi ran up to her and handed her a mango, his eyes twinkling. "Come, Amma, sit with us. Let's eat together!"

Radhamma took the mango, feeling the warmth of the children's presence wrap around her. She sat down on the cot, watching them as they devoured the mangoes, laughing and talking. The house felt alive once more, filled with the sound of children, the way it had been years ago.

As the afternoon wore on, the children urged her to tell them stories. Radhamma, who had spent years gathering tales from her own childhood and village life, began to tell them stories of the old days. Her voice, though soft, was clear, and the children listened with wide eyes, enraptured. She told them of the festivals they used to celebrate, the traditions they followed, and the games they played in the fields. Her words painted vivid pictures of a time when life was slower, simpler, and filled with joy.

As she spoke, Ravi watched her, noticing the light in her eyes, the way her face softened as she remembered those days. He felt a sense of pride, knowing that he had been able to bring her a little happiness. And in that moment, he made a silent promise to himself—to look after Radhamma, to be there for her in the way her family could not.

That evening, as the sun dipped below the horizon and the children prepared to leave, Radhamma felt a warmth in her heart she hadn't felt in a long time. She watched them go, waving until they were out of sight. And as she turned to go back inside, she felt a sense of contentment, knowing that she was not alone, that there were still people who cared for her.

For the first time in years, Radhamma didn't feel the weight of waiting. She knew her grandchildren might never come, that the demands of city life had drawn them away. But as she looked at the mango trees, laden with fruit, she felt a renewed sense of purpose. She would continue to tend to them, to care for them, knowing that she had found a new family in the children of the village.

And as she sat on her cot, gazing at the stars, Radhamma knew that her waiting was over. She had found joy in unexpected places, in the laughter of children, in the warmth of companionship. And that, she realized, was enough.

The days after the children's visit brought a renewed energy to Radhamma's life. Every morning, she found herself humming as she swept the courtyard and checked the ripening mangoes, which seemed to glow brighter and smell sweeter than ever. The memories of her laughter-filled home had once felt like ghosts, but now they were vivid again, present in every corner, and all because of Ravi and the other children. They had filled her heart with a joy that she hadn't thought possible in her old age.

Word spread quickly through the village of Radhamma's happiness, of how the children had filled her home with their presence, and soon enough, other neighbours and passersby began stopping by. Some would come to check on her, while others would linger in her courtyard, chatting about village news, sharing stories, and accepting a mango or two from her generous hands. Radhamma's home had become a place of gathering, a place where laughter and conversation found refuge, a place that felt like the heart of the village.

But, true to his nature, it was Ravi who visited the most. He came every other day, sometimes with friends, sometimes alone, and he always brought his radiant smile. He would come bounding through the gate, calling out, "Amma! Do you have any mangoes today?" as if the house would run out of them overnight.

One bright afternoon, as Radhamma was spreading a fresh batch of mangoes to dry for pickling, she spotted Ravi strolling up the path. This time, he wasn't alone. He was accompanied by a few other village children—Lakshmi, Sundar, little Sita with her big curious eyes, and Murugan, his best friend. The group ambled in, and each child called out a cheerful greeting.

"Come in, come in," Radhamma said, waving them toward the courtyard with an excited gleam in her eyes.

"I have some ripe ones here, fresh from the trees this morning."

They gathered around her, eagerly grabbing the mangoes she handed them. Ravi picked one up and tossed it between his hands, then bit into it, juice dripping down his chin. He grinned widely, not bothering to wipe his face. "Amma, I don't think anyone in the world can grow mangoes like you!"

Radhamma chuckled, swatting at him with her wrinkled hand. "Ah, it's the soil, boy, and maybe a bit of love," she said. "These trees have been here longer than you or me. They're my family too, in a way."

The children glanced at each other, puzzled. To them, trees were just trees. But Ravi, as usual, was intrigued.

"How can a tree be family, Amma?" he asked, genuine curiosity in his eyes.

Radhamma looked at the towering mango tree beside them, her expression softening. "These trees have been here since my husband and I first came to this land. We planted them together, watered them, watched them grow. I used to talk to them when I was lonely, tell them my troubles, and they would sway as if listening. They've seen me through every season, every joy and sorrow. Isn't that what family does?"

The children nodded solemnly, moved by her words, even though they couldn't fully understand them. But Ravi did. Ravi had always sensed there was something more to life's simple things, something worth holding onto.

"Amma," he said, after a moment's thought, "then that means we're family too, doesn't it? We'll keep coming here, just like these trees. We won't let you be alone."

Radhamma's heart filled with warmth. She felt, perhaps for the first time in years, a genuine connection that reached beyond blood ties. Ravi and these children were indeed like family to her now. And the sincerity in Ravi's words—his promise to come back—resonated in a way that healed the ache in her heart just a little more.

As they sat in companionable silence, Sundar piped up, "Amma, will you teach us how to make that mango pickle everyone talks about?"

Radhamma's eyes sparkled. "Oh, so you want to know my secrets, do you?" she teased, but the joy in her voice gave her away. "Very well, but you must follow my instructions carefully. Pickle-making is an art, you know."

The children sat up, attentive, as Radhamma began explaining the intricate steps of preparing mango pickle. She spoke of selecting the right mangoes—ones that were neither too ripe nor too green. She showed them how to slice them into perfect pieces, evenly sized so they would absorb the spices just right. Then, she took them through the process of mixing the ingredients—the turmeric, the red chili powder, the salt, and the carefully measured oil.

"Every family has its own way," she explained as she demonstrated the technique, her hands deftly moving with years of practice. "But this recipe has been passed down through my family for generations."

Ravi, watching her keenly, absorbed every word, nodding along as though committing each step to memory. "Amma, one day, I'll make pickle just like this. And then I'll bring it to you to taste."

Radhamma laughed, her heart swelling with pride. "Then I shall be the judge of your skills," she said with a mock-serious tone, wagging her finger at him. "But you must remember that the secret to good pickle is patience. You must let it sit and soak up the spices. Just like people, it needs time to become its best self."

The children worked alongside her, slicing mangoes, mixing ingredients, and laughing as they sprinkled too much salt or stirred too vigorously, resulting in a small splash of oil here and there. Radhamma didn't mind the mess; in fact, she relished every moment. Her courtyard felt like a workshop, alive with learning and laughter, and her heart brimmed with a sense of purpose she hadn't felt in years.

As evening drew near, the children packed up the pickle they'd made under her guidance, each taking a small portion to their own homes, proudly declaring that they would "feed it to their families and tell them it was Radhamma's recipe."

Before leaving, Ravi looked at her earnestly. "Amma, we'll come back soon, won't we?"

Radhamma smiled, brushing a few crumbs of dried chili powder off her hands. "Of course, Ravi. You're welcome any time."

And so began a new rhythm to Radhamma's life. Every few days, the children would come to visit her, sometimes for pickle-making, other times simply to sit with her and share stories. Ravi continued to visit most frequently, always with new questions and a genuine interest in the world she described. To him, the stories of

Radhamma's youth—of the village festivals, the harvest dances, and the ways of life now forgotten—were tales of wonder, as fascinating as any adventure.

One afternoon, Ravi arrived at her house with a serious look on his face. He sat beside Radhamma and handed her a piece of paper folded carefully.

"What's this, Ravi?" she asked, unfolding it gently.

"It's a letter for your grandchildren, Amma," he replied. "I thought that maybe, if they knew how much you missed them, they'd come to visit."

Radhamma looked down at the letter, her heart caught between hope and sadness. She read Ravi's neat handwriting, the words simple yet heartfelt. He had written about how Radhamma waited for them each year, how she prepared the house, the food, the mangoes, all with the hope of their arrival. He had even mentioned how she had taught them all to make mango pickle, "her special family recipe," as he put it.

She looked at Ravi, her eyes misty. "You're a good boy, Ravi. But they're busy, you see. City life… it changes people."

Ravi shook his head. "But, Amma, you always say that family is like these mango trees. They're strong and rooted. They may bend with the wind, but they don't break."

Radhamma felt a lump in her throat, but she managed to smile. "You're right, Ravi. Perhaps they'll come next year. And if they don't, well… I have you all, don't I?"

Ravi grinned, a smile that seemed to hold all the loyalty and love a young heart could offer. "Yes, Amma. We'll be here. We're not going anywhere."

The letter was left unposted, tucked safely in Radhamma's chest of old belongings. She knew her grandchildren would come when they were ready, in their own time.

Until then, she was content with the family she had found in the children of her village. They had filled her days with laughter, her heart with love, and her home with life.

And as the last batch of the season's mangoes was yet to be harvested, Radhamma looked at her beloved trees and smiled, still hoping for the best.

The last batch of mangoes brought an unexpected surprise to Radhamma's doorstep. As the mango trees began their final flourish of the year, filling the air with their heady fragrance, Radhamma busied herself with the familiar routines of harvest. She carefully picked and sorted the fruits, setting aside the ripest ones for Ravi and his friends, who had by now become a fixture in her life. The previous weeks had cemented a bond between her and the village children, one that grew with each passing day, filling her memories with the kind of joy and companionship she had thought lost to her.

One particularly hot afternoon, as Radhamma was hanging mango slices to dry under the sun for another batch of pickles, she heard the sound of footsteps—a cautious, hesitant kind, not like the boisterous footfalls of Ravi and his gang. She peered out from the doorway, her heart beating a little faster, a pang of hope rising within her that she tried to quash, for disappointment had become too familiar.

But there they were. Her son, his wife, and her grandchildren stood at the gate, shaded by the large mango trees, looking slightly out of place yet unmistakably there. For a moment, Radhamma thought she was imagining them. She blinked, gripping the doorframe for support, before calling out in a voice that quavered with emotion.

"Ramu, is it really you?" she said, her voice barely a whisper.

Her son smiled—a little sheepishly, a little guiltily—and nodded. "Yes, Amma, it's us."

With that confirmation, Radhamma's heart flooded with an overwhelming mix of joy and relief. Her grandchildren, whom she had last seen as little children with gapped smiles and eager, sticky fingers, now stood before her as teenagers, taller and leaner, with an air of confidence and city life about them. But she didn't dwell on the changes; they were here, and that was all that mattered.

Radhamma welcomed them in, her old eyes misting as she held each of them close. The house, which had recently echoed with the laughter of village children, now felt alive in a different way. Her family was here— her family, for whom she had waited through many summers, her family, who had finally come home.

Over the next few days, Radhamma's house transformed. Ramu and his wife, Sita, took to the village life with surprising ease, though they marvelled at the simplicity of it. The children, who had initially been quiet and hesitant, soon found their rhythm, exploring the house and the courtyard, climbing the mango trees, and even making friends with Ravi and the other village children. Ravi, who had first spotted the family's arrival, had brought news of it to the entire village, and in typical fashion, had already bonded with Radhamma's grandchildren, introducing them to the village and sharing with them the secrets of Radhamma's beloved trees.

One afternoon, Radhamma's eldest granddaughter, Priya, came to her, holding a partially ripe mango that had fallen from the tree. "Paati," she began, using the Tamil term for grandmother, "did you really teach all the village children how to make mango pickle?"

Radhamma chuckled, nodding. "Oh, yes! They've been coming here for weeks, helping me with the pickles. You know, it was Ravi who insisted I teach them. He said everyone should know the family recipe!"

The girl looked at her, fascinated. "Will you teach me too?"

Radhamma's heart swelled as she led Priya and her younger brother, Arjun, to the back of the house, where she had arranged the jars and spices for her pickle-making. They spent hours together, Radhamma showing them each step, correcting their slices, and laughing as they made mistakes. Priya and Arjun took to the work eagerly, their laughter mingling with Radhamma's as they tasted the raw mangoes, wincing at the sourness, and trying to follow her instructions as best they could.

Watching her grandchildren handle the mangoes with careful hands, Radhamma felt as if a circle in her life was finally closing. The family recipe, the traditions she had guarded, the love she had poured into each jar of pickle—it was now being passed on, as naturally as the seasons turning, as enduring as her beloved trees.

That evening, when the pickle-making was done, Radhamma gathered her family around and brought out a large basket of ripe mangoes. They ate together under the open sky, sticky fingers and laughter filling the courtyard as dusk settled over the village. Her son looked at her, a thoughtful expression crossing his face.

"Amma, I've missed this," he said quietly. "I didn't realize how much until now. Life in the city, it's… it's different. I had forgotten how simple things like this used to make me happy."

Radhamma placed a hand on his arm, her voice soft. "The city has its ways, Ramu, and the village has its own. But remember, this home is always here for you. These trees... they've been waiting too, you know."

Her son looked at her, understanding what she meant. He glanced at the mango trees, their thick trunks standing tall and firm, roots deep in the soil. In their quiet presence, he sensed the same permanence, the same enduring love that Radhamma had nurtured all these years.

As the days went by, Ramu and his family began to consider their visits to the village as more than a passing novelty. They lingered, soaking in the simplicity, the unhurried pace of life, the warmth of the people. Sita, who had always considered village life quaint and perhaps even a little dull, found herself enchanted by Radhamma's stories and wisdom, realizing the depth and richness of a life connected to the land, to family, and to traditions.

But it was the children who were most transformed by their time with Radhamma and the village children. They became fast friends with Ravi and his gang, learning village games, running through the fields, even swimming in the small river nearby. For Priya and Arjun, these experiences were a revelation, a world away from their life in the city, and they often stayed up late, talking with Radhamma about her own childhood, wanting to hear more of the life she had led.

On the last evening of their visit, as the family prepared to leave the next day, Ravi and the other village children gathered at Radhamma's house for a small farewell. They brought small gifts for her—mangoes they had picked, flowers, a few fresh vegetables from their families' fields, tokens of the affection they felt for her. Ravi, as always, was at the forefront, though this time, his usually cheerful face looked downcast.

"Amma," Ramu said quietly as he stood by her side "we'll miss you."

Radhamma looked at him, her own heart heavy. She had grown used to his presence, endless questions from the children, and the laughter. She patted his cheek gently. "I'll miss you too, Ramu. But you know where I am, don't you? This house, this land—it's as much yours as it is mine. The mango trees here will be awaiting your visit every year."

With that, she handed Ramu a small jar of the mango pickle he loved so much, wrapped carefully in a cloth. "Take this. It'll remind you of me until you come back."

Ramu's face brightened, and he accepted the jar as if it were a treasure. The next morning, Radhamma stood at the gate, waving goodbye as Ramu and his family climbed into the car, their own arms laden with jars of pickle, baskets of mangoes, and Radhamma's heartfelt reminders to return soon. The ache of parting was softened by the knowledge that this time, they would come back, that her house would not remain empty, her heart not hollow. As the car disappeared down the dusty road, Ravi appeared at her side, his presence as familiar as the trees around her. He looked up at her, a quiet promise in his eyes. "Amma," he said, his voice full of conviction, "we'll take care of you. Your family and us, we'll always be here." Radhamma looked at him, her heart swelling with gratitude and pride. She placed a hand on his shoulder, her touch gentle, firm. "Thank you, Ravi. You've given me more than you know."

She watched him run back toward the village, feeling a sense of peace that settled deep within her. Her family had found their way back to her, and even in their absence, she had a new family that loved her just as dearly.

The seasons would come and go, the mangoes would ripen and fall, but Radhamma knew that she would never be alone again. In the embrace of her beloved trees, in the laughter of village children, in the footsteps of those she loved, her heart would remain full, her waiting finally rewarded.

The Temple Keeper's Secret

In the bustling heart of Chennai, where the old-world charm mingled with the cacophony of modernity, stood an ancient temple. Its walls were worn with time, each crack and crevice a testament to the whispers of centuries past. Nestled between towering apartment buildings and encroaching storefronts, this temple was an anachronism—a quiet shrine to memory in a city racing forward. Here, Krishnamurthy, an elderly man with silvered hair and a face mapped by a lifetime of smiles and sorrow, served as its keeper.

Krishnamurthy was more than a caretaker. To those who frequented the temple, he was a sage, a friend, and a custodian of stories. His appearance had changed little over the years—a faded dhoti, neatly draped paired with his loyal walking stick. He was tall and thin, with a slightly bent back that had long borne the weight of both reverence and responsibility. His eyes, though faded, held a spark that could only be kindled by a love for history and the divine.

The temple, as Krishnamurthy was fond of recounting, had been built over long time ago, as the legend goes, by a wandering saint who, some said, had received a vision. The vision instructed him to lay the foundation for a shrine that would honour the benevolence of the gods and provide refuge for those who sought solace. Over time, this temple had grown into a cherished landmark, attracting devotees from far and wide. But, as the years passed, the modern world had begun to encroach, and fewer pilgrims came, preferring the larger, glitzier temples in the city. The once-bustling grounds now saw only a handful of visitors, and the offerings were fewer.

Krishnamurthy, however, remained unfazed by the lack of crowds. Each morning, he arrived before sunrise, sweeping the grounds, lighting the lamps, and preparing the deities for the day. He worked slowly, almost reverently, taking time to mutter an occasional prayer as his broom traced the same path each day.

One day, as he was tidying the outer courtyard, a young man in a crisp white shirt approached him. His clothes, his confident gait, and the shiny leather bag he carried all screamed of the corporate world.

"Krishnamurthy," the man greeted him with an air of familiarity that was mildly irritating.

"Yes?" Krishnamurthy looked up, squinting slightly in the early morning sun.

"My name is Sundar. I represent Platinum Developers. We've been trying to get in touch with you."

Krishnamurthy's heart skipped a beat. He had heard rumours of developers eyeing the temple land. The news had trickled in through whispers among the neighbourhood vendors and brief remarks from the local gossip. But he'd chosen to ignore them, treating them as idle talk. Now, confronted by this man, the truth struck like a gong in the still morning air.

"We are planning a major project—a shopping complex with all the modern amenities. You see, the city is expanding, and this area is prime real estate. We think it could do well for the people around here, too, bringing jobs and opportunity." Sundar spoke with an air of polished rehearsals, his words as slick as his gelled hair.

Krishnamurthy stayed silent, his hand gripping his walking stick a bit more tightly. He was a man of few words, and this wasn't a conversation he wanted.

"The temple," Sundar continued, unfazed by Krishnamurthy's silence, "is part of the proposed site. But don't worry—we have plans for it. We want to keep it intact, maybe incorporate it into the design of the shopping complex. A bit of heritage, you know? It could add charm."

The idea of his beloved temple being reduced to a decorative feature in a shopping mall sent a chill down Krishnamurthy's spine.

"Sir," Krishnamurthy's voice was low, his words carefully chosen. "This temple is not just stones and statues. It is a place of spirit, of devotion. It cannot be moved, nor can it be changed."

Sundar laughed lightly, as if amused by the old man's insistence. "I understand, sir. Tradition is important to you. But times are changing, and we must change with them." His tone softened, and he added, "Please consider this. We will compensate everyone fairly. We are not here to destroy, only to progress."

With that, he handed Krishnamurthy a business card and departed, his polished shoes clicking against the stone steps.

Krishnamurthy remained rooted to his spot, watching the young man walk away. The morning sun, warm and bright, did nothing to ease the chill spreading within him. He turned back to the temple, his gaze drifting to the towering sanctum, where the deity resided, serene and unmoved by the world's turmoil.

It was then, for the first time in many years, that Krishnamurthy felt the weight of the secret he had been entrusted with. His mind drifted to a day many years ago, when his predecessor, Venkataraman, had called him into the innermost sanctum of the temple. Venkataraman was an old man then, his body frail but his mind sharp.

"Krishna," Venkataraman had whispered, "one day, you will need to protect this temple. Not just from vandals or thieves, but from those who believe they know what is best. They will come with big promises and talk of progress, but remember, some things must remain untouched. And when that day comes, you must know how to keep the temple safe."

Venkataraman had led him to the back of the sanctum, where a small, unassuming door lay hidden behind faded surroundings. With a quivering hand, the old man had pushed the door open, revealing a dimly lit chamber. At the centre lay a large, intricately carved stone slab, and on it was etched a symbol Krishnamurthy had never seen before. Venkataraman had told him then of a power hidden within the temple grounds, a source of energy that could protect the temple if ever it was in danger.

Krishnamurthy had been sceptical then, dismissing it as a tale crafted to instil reverence. But now, with Sundar's words ringing in his ears, he began to wonder if Venkataraman's words had been more than an old man's ramblings.

Over the next few days, Sundar returned several times, each visit more insistent than the last. Krishnamurthy found himself cornered, his peaceful world disrupted by endless negotiations and promises. Sundar's voice was relentless, echoing through the temple walls even when he wasn't there.

Finally, on the seventh day, as Sundar made yet another attempt, Krishnamurthy took him aside. "There is a place," he began, his voice low, "that not many know of, inside the temple."

Sundar raised an eyebrow, curiosity piqued. "A hidden chamber?"

"Yes," Krishnamurthy said, choosing his words carefully. "If you are sincere in your desire to understand this temple, then you should see it."

Intrigued, Sundar followed him. As they passed through the narrow corridors and entered the innermost sanctum, Sundar's polished confidence began to wane. There was a stillness here, an air of reverence that even his modern sensibilities couldn't ignore.

Krishnamurthy led him to the small door hidden behind the tapestry and opened it, revealing the chamber. Sundar stepped in, his eyes widening as he took in the carvings and symbols etched into the stone slab.

"This," Krishnamurthy said, his voice soft, "is the soul of the temple. It has watched over this place for centuries, guarding it. If you take away the temple, you will take away this soul."

Sundar stared at the carvings, a flicker of awe crossing his face. But his voice was uncertain. "How does this stop progress, Krishnamurthy? This is impressive, yes. But it's just... history. Progress must respect the past, but it must move forward."

Krishnamurthy felt his heart sink. The young man's words echoed with a harshness, a certainty that left no room for compromise. He had shown him the temple's deepest secret, hoping it would ignite a sense of reverence. But in Sundar's eyes, he saw only the shimmer of profit and opportunity.

As Sundar walked out, Krishnamurthy remained in the chamber, the dim light casting shadows across the carvings. He placed a trembling hand on the stone slab, feeling the weight of generations pressing down upon him.

Days turned into weeks, and Krishnamurthy found himself entangled in an ongoing battle with Sundar and the developers. Their promises grew grander, their arguments more persuasive. Krishnamurthy, however, stood firm, his resolve becoming as unyielding as the temple walls themselves. But as he watched the city's towering glass and steel encroach ever closer, his heart grew heavy with the realization that his quiet resistance alone might not be enough.

One evening, Krishnamurthy sat on the temple steps, gazing at the street where the vendors sold garlands, incense sticks, and clay lamps. The aroma of jasmine and camphor mingled with the evening air, filling him with a bittersweet nostalgia. He was deep in thought when a voice called out to him.

"Krishna Mama!" It was Anbu, a bright-eyed boy from the neighbourhood who often ran errands for him. Anbu was a familiar presence, as loyal to the temple as its most devout patrons.

"Yes, Anbu," Krishnamurthy replied, his voice soft but warm.

Anbu sat beside him, dangling his legs off the steps. "Mama, I heard the men talking. They say the temple will be turned into a shop soon. Is it true?"

Krishnamurthy sighed. He wanted to tell Anbu it was just a rumour, but the boy's earnest face left him unable to speak anything but the truth.

"There are people who want to make changes, Anbu. They believe it will bring more money and more people to the area. But not all changes are good," he said, his voice laced with a sadness that Anbu didn't miss.

Anbu's face grew serious. "Mama, if the temple goes, where will the people go to pray?"

Krishnamurthy placed a gentle hand on the boy's shoulder. "That's what I am trying to stop, Anbu. Sometimes, we have to protect what is sacred, even when others can't see its worth."

Anbu looked up, his eyes wide with determination. "Mama, if you need help, I will help you. My friends and I—we all love the temple. We will do whatever you ask."

Krishnamurthy felt a surge of warmth in his heart. The boy's loyalty reminded him of his younger self, when he too had first come to the temple as an assistant. He knew that the power of faith wasn't merely in rituals or offerings but in the spirit of those who cherished these sacred spaces.

But as the days passed, it became clear that faith alone might not be enough. Sundar returned with blueprints, legal papers, and endless talk of profits and progress. And though Krishnamurthy tried to engage him with stories of the temple's history and significance, his words fell on ears deafened by ambition.

One evening, Sundar arrived with a larger entourage—men in dark suits with serious faces. The temple grounds, usually quiet and serene in the evenings, filled with a sense of foreboding as the men walked around, inspecting every corner with calculating eyes. Krishnamurthy's heart raced as they began discussing floor plans and allocations, treating the temple like a parcel of land rather than a sacred space.

Finally, Krishnamurthy could take it no longer. As the group reached the main sanctum, he stepped forward and raised his voice. "Stop this at once!"

Sundar turned, visibly irritated. "Krishnamurthy, we've been through this. The decision is made. I am here to finalize the plans, not to debate."

"The decision is not yours to make!" Krishnamurthy's voice quivered with a mix of anger and desperation. "This temple has stood here for centuries, protected by the faith of those who worship here. You cannot tear it down for a few rupees."

Sundar shook his head, a weary smile on his face. "I don't expect you to understand, Krishnamurthy. This is progress, and it is inevitable. You are clinging to the past, but the world is moving on."

With that, he and his entourage exited the temple, leaving Krishnamurthy standing alone in the sanctum, his heart pounding. He felt as if he had failed, as if the temple's fate was slipping from his grasp.

As darkness descended, Krishnamurthy found himself in the hidden chamber once more, tracing his fingers over the ancient carvings. The cool stone beneath his hand felt like a tether, grounding him in his purpose. He closed his eyes, recalling Venkataraman's words, and a thought began to take root in his mind.

"If this temple is meant to be protected," he murmured to himself, "then there must be a way."

The next morning, Krishnamurthy gathered Anbu and a few others from the neighbourhood who had grown up visiting the temple. They were young, fiery, and determined, ready to stand with him against the developers. Together, they set up a watch at the temple gates, politely asking visitors to sign a petition against the demolition. Word spread quickly, and before long, the temple grounds were filled with people—students, elders, families—all united in their desire to save the shrine.

News of the movement reached the press, and reporters came to document the temple's plight. Krishnamurthy spoke with a quiet dignity, sharing the temple's history and the secret that lay within its walls, though he left out the exact details of the hidden chamber. The media coverage brought more supporters, and for a moment, Krishnamurthy felt a glimmer of hope.

But Sundar was not easily deterred. As the movement gained momentum, he met with Krishnamurthy privately one afternoon, hoping to appeal to his sense of practicality.

"Look, Krishnamurthy," Sundar began, "I respect your dedication to this temple, but this opposition is only going to slow down the inevitable. If you agree to cooperate, we can create something that preserves the essence of the temple, even if the structure itself is changed."

Krishnamurthy shook his head, his expression resolute. "The essence of the temple is in its foundation, its very stones. To remove even a part of it would be to destroy its spirit. You may not understand, Sundar, but some things must remain untouched if they are to retain their power."

Sundar exhaled sharply, frustration flashing in his eyes. "Very well, then. But know that we will proceed as planned, with or without your support."

Krishnamurthy watched him go, his heart sinking. He had known this fight would not be easy, but the reality of Sundar's words hit him like a blow.

The next day, as Krishnamurthy walked through the temple grounds, he noticed a crowd gathered near the gate. To his surprise, an elderly woman, frail but fierce, stood at the centre of the gathering, clutching a walking stick.

"Krishna Mama!" she called out when she saw him, her face lighting up with recognition. She was none other than Ammu, a devout woman who had visited the temple daily for years before moving away.

"Ammu!" Krishnamurthy greeted her, his voice filled with warmth. "What brings you here?"

"I heard of the trouble," Ammu said, her voice steady. "And I couldn't sit by and watch this temple, my temple, be taken from us."

Krishnamurthy felt a swell of emotion as Ammu raised her voice, addressing the crowd. "This temple is not just a building! It is our sanctuary, a place where generations have come to find peace. If they take this from us, they take away our heritage, our very soul."

The crowd cheered, and Krishnamurthy felt a surge of hope. This was no longer just his fight. It was the fight of every soul who cherished the temple. Ammu's words spread through the community like wildfire, and soon more people arrived, each carrying a story, a memory, or a prayer. The temple grounds swelled with life once more, as though the very walls were invigorated by the voices that called for its preservation.

But Sundar was not easily deterred. He arrived at the temple that evening with a court order in hand, accompanied by police and a small team of workers. He addressed the crowd with cool indifference, brandishing the document like a weapon.

"This temple is now the property of Platinum Developers," he declared. "Those who resist will be removed by force if necessary."

A hush fell over the crowd as Krishnamurthy stepped forward, his hands clasped in prayer. His voice, calm yet firm, rang out above the murmurs.

"I may be an old man," he said, "but I am willing to lay down my life to protect this temple. And I am not alone."

A murmur of agreement swept through the crowd as others stepped forward to stand beside him. Anbu, Ammu, and dozens of others formed a human chain around the temple, their expressions unwavering. Sundar's face tightened, and for the first time, a flicker of uncertainty crossed his eyes.

As the sun began to set, casting a golden light over the temple grounds, Krishnamurthy felt a strange calm settle over him. He knew that this was only the beginning, and that the battle ahead would test every ounce of his faith. But in that moment, he stood tall, resolute, with the power of generations behind him and the spirit of the temple pulsing through his veins.

The standoff continued through the night. The crowd that surrounded the temple remained steadfast, unwilling to yield. By morning, the streets were filled with supporters—families, elderly residents, young professionals, and even students from nearby colleges. They held lamps, sang bhajans, and prayed, filling the air with a quiet strength that even the police presence seemed reluctant to disturb. Krishnamurthy watched, heart swelling, as people from all walks of life joined together in defiance of the developers.

Sundar, however, was not one to be outmanoeuvred. By mid-morning, he was back, frustration etched deep in his face. He gestured to the police, who reluctantly began to approach the crowd. Krishnamurthy saw them coming and took a deep breath, feeling the weight of the moment settle on him like a heavy shroud.

"Krishnamurthy," Sundar called out, his voice carrying a note of warning. "This is the final chance. Disperse this crowd, and we will arrange a dignified relocation for the temple's sanctum. This gathering is illegal, and I will not hesitate to call in more force."

Krishnamurthy looked around at the faces beside him—Anbu, Ammu, and the many others who had come to protect the temple. With a deep, calming breath, he stepped forward, his voice carrying over the noise.

"Sundar, you may have the law on your side, but you do not have what matters most—the spirit of this temple and the faith of the people who come here." He raised a trembling hand, pointing toward the sanctum. "You can take the walls, the statues, the stones, but you cannot take the heart of this place. The heart of this temple is not something you can see or touch. It is in the prayers, the faith, and the love of everyone here."

Sundar's expression softened, if only for a moment, as he glanced at the crowd. But he was a man bound by duty and ambition, and he turned away, giving the signal to his workers. They began to advance with tools and machinery, ready to dismantle the structure piece by piece.

As the first worker stepped forward, Krishnamurthy knew it was time. He turned to the hidden chamber within the sanctum, where the stone slab lay. He had been entrusted with its secret by his predecessor, and in this desperate hour, he felt compelled to use the knowledge passed down to him. He motioned to Anbu, who followed him with wide, curious eyes as they entered the inner sanctum.

"Anbu, listen carefully," Krishnamurthy whispered. "This is a place of great power, something that our ancestors left here to protect the temple. I don't fully understand its nature, but I know it will help us."

With a sense of solemnity, Krishnamurthy placed his hands on the stone slab and closed his eyes, murmuring the ancient chant his predecessor had taught him. His voice, though soft, seemed to carry through the air, blending with the quiet hum of the crowd outside. He prayed, not just with words but with every fibre of his being, for the temple's safety and for the people who cherished it.

Anbu watched, eyes wide with awe, as the symbols on the stone slab seemed to faintly glow under the dim oil lamp, casting a soft, golden light across the chamber. A gentle tremor seemed to ripple through the temple walls, as though the very earth was responding to Krishnamurthy's plea.

Outside, the crowd noticed the subtle change. The air grew thick, almost electric, and a hush fell over the gathering. Sundar's workers paused, hesitating as the ground beneath them seemed to shift ever so slightly. The faint tremor was not violent, but it was enough to make even the most resolute among them question whether it was wise to continue.

Sundar looked around, bewildered, as his workers stepped back, fear flickering in their eyes. "What are you doing? It's just an old building!" he shouted, but his voice was lost amidst the stillness that had descended like a shroud.

Krishnamurthy emerged from the sanctum, his face calm and his stance firm. His presence seemed to radiate a quiet strength, a deep connection to the place he had devoted his life to. He approached Sundar, who stood frozen, his confidence shaken.

"Sundar," Krishnamurthy said, his voice steady but kind, "you have seen for yourself that this temple is not just a structure. It holds a power that you cannot touch or control. It was built to protect, to heal, and to bring peace to those who come here. I beg you, for the sake of all that is sacred, to leave it as it is."

Sundar looked around, the realization dawning on him that he was no longer in control. The workers had already begun to retreat, muttering nervously among themselves. The police officers, too, looked uncertain, as though sensing a force beyond their understanding. And the crowd, united in its silent prayer, seemed to form an impenetrable wall, standing guard over the temple.

Defeated, Sundar nodded, his shoulders slumping as he accepted that this was a battle he could not win. "Very well, Krishnamurthy," he said, his voice barely a whisper. "The temple will remain as it is."

A wave of relief washed over the crowd, and a cheer rose up, filling the air with joy and gratitude. People embraced, their faces shining with a shared sense of triumph and reverence. Krishnamurthy felt a tear slip

down his cheek, though he quickly brushed it away. He had protected the temple, not through force but through faith and the bond he shared with those around him.

As the crowd slowly dispersed, Anbu approached him, his young face filled with admiration. "Mama, was that...was that magic?"

Krishnamurthy chuckled softly, resting a hand on the boy's shoulder. "It was the power of faith, Anbu. Faith that has been here for generations, passed down from one keeper to another. It's a power that cannot be bought or sold, and it will always protect those who believe."

With Sundar and his team gone, Krishnamurthy walked through the temple, pausing to touch the walls, to feel the cool stone beneath his fingers. He thought of his predecessors, of Venkataraman, and all those who had come before him, each one leaving a piece of themselves in the very heart of the temple.

As the evening set in, the temple returned to its usual, serene self, the flickering oil lamps casting a warm glow over the sanctum. Krishnamurthy felt at peace, knowing that he had fulfilled his duty as a keeper, not only of the temple but of its spirit. The hidden chamber, the secret, the power—they would remain here, waiting for the next generation, for the next keeper who would protect it when the time came.

As he made his way back to his small quarters near the temple, Krishnamurthy looked up at the sky, a silent prayer of gratitude on his lips. He was only one in a long line of guardians, but he knew that he had done his part, and that the temple, the heart of his life, would continue to stand as a beacon of faith and tradition for all who came after him.

In the silence of the night, the temple watched over the city, its ancient spirit undisturbed and unwavering, there stood the piling machine across the road that had been digging earth earlier and caused the gentle tremor, a reminder that support is always given at the opportune moment even through inanimate things, when there is timeless strength found in faith and the enduring power of those who choose to protect it.

A Saree For Amma

The village of Periya Vaikal sat quietly along the Bay of Bengal, tucked away from the bustling world beyond, breathing in sync with the waves that lapped its shore. It was the sort of place where people lived simply, their lives woven with the tide, the monsoon, and the seasons of fishing. Here, the thatched roofs leaned into each other, forming narrow lanes, and coconut trees cast swaying shadows on old walls. In the heart of this village lived Lakshmi, a widow of quiet fortitude who managed her household alone. Her children had grown, some flown away to distant cities, others remaining closer, though wrapped in their own lives.

Lakshmi's daughter, Nila, was still in the village, busy with her own young family. Though Nila visited often, Lakshmi noticed a distance, a shift she could neither name nor shake. Lakshmi, now past sixty, found herself surrounded by silence—interrupted only by the sounds of cooking or an occasional visitor. Yet there was one voice that still filled the spaces of her home, an echo of the past: her mother's voice. In the quiet of dawn or the dimming evening, Lakshmi could still hear Amma's soft laugh, the rattle of her bangles, the words of gentle wisdom she'd shared over the years.

One day, as she sat by the small window watching the afternoon sun glint off the blue sea, Lakshmi was overtaken by a memory of her mother. She saw her as clear as day: Amma standing in her garden, her saree—a vibrant indigo cotton with a thin zari border—draped impeccably over her shoulder, the free end tucked under her arm as she patted the heads of the children who'd come to listen to her stories. Amma had a way of making everyone feel loved, drawing them in like a mother hen.

Lakshmi reached into her chest, feeling a tug that had long been buried under years of routine.

That evening, as the street lamps flickered on and women called their children indoors, Lakshmi found herself crossing the village toward Rajarathnam Chettiar's sari shop. She hadn't entered the shop in ages, the last time being to buy a wedding sari for her daughter. The shop had been there since her mother's time, a small wonder in itself, for shops rarely survived the march of years. Its wooden sign was freshly painted, and the narrow interior glowed under a single, muted bulb. There, stacks of sarees leaned against each other on shelves that groaned with age, like the memories Lakshmi herself had stacked inside her heart.

The old shopkeeper smiled when he saw her enter, his glasses perched on the end of his nose, hands folded in a respectful greeting.

"Ah, Lakshmi-amma! It has been a long time. How can I help you today?"

Lakshmi hesitated, her words caught somewhere between her heart and her throat. "I am looking for a saree... one like my Amma used to wear," she finally said, a faint blush colouring her cheeks. She was a woman well past the age of blushes, yet here she was, feeling as shy as a young girl. "A simple one... indigo, if you have it."

Chettiar's eyes sparkled with understanding. He knew the saree she was speaking of; he remembered her mother, the woman who was a presence in the village, always warm, always composed. He shuffled to the back of the shop and pulled out a saree wrapped in tissue, carefully unwinding the fabric. It was a deep indigo with a thin, golden border that shimmered subtly in the light.

Lakshmi's fingers brushed over the cloth, and she felt a rush of emotions she hadn't anticipated. The soft cotton against her fingertips was like a thread to the past, as if touching it brought her closer to her mother. Her Amma's memory filled the room, vibrant and alive, breathing life into the folds of the fabric.

"This will do," she murmured, her voice trembling slightly. She gathered the saree to her chest, holding it close as if it were a cherished memory, paying without haggling, and left the shop in a haze of nostalgia and unexpected joy.

At home, she laid the saree out on her bed and simply stared at it. The house was quiet; even the kitchen seemed to have stilled, as though sensing the significance of the moment. She lifted the saree and draped it over herself, clumsily at first, her fingers feeling unfamiliar with the act after so many years of wearing simpler, less vibrant colours. But as the saree settled over her shoulders and around her waist, she felt a strange warmth, as though Amma herself had wrapped her arms around her.

Just then, Nila entered, her voice light with laughter until she saw her mother. She stopped short, her gaze resting on Lakshmi, her eyes wide with surprise and something else—something she couldn't quite place. For a fleeting moment, she felt as if she were staring at her grandmother, a vision from her childhood, of a woman who had stood firm as a banyan tree, her love sheltering all who sought her shade. Nila's laughter faded, replaced by a quiet respect and a new awareness that seemed to bridge the distance between her and her mother.

"Amma," Nila murmured, taking a hesitant step forward. "You look… you look just like Paati."

Lakshmi's face softened, her heart swelling with the bittersweet comfort of memory. She reached out to Nila, pulling her close. "Sometimes I miss her, Nila. She's with me, I feel her around me, in every corner of this house. But today, I wanted to feel her here," she said, patting her heart. "It felt like a piece of her came back with me today."

Nila said nothing, but her eyes shimmered with understanding. She hadn't thought of her mother in this way, hadn't seen her as anything but the woman who had always been there to cook, clean, care. And here she was, looking at Lakshmi as if seeing her for the first time— a woman who had known loss, love, and the quiet strength of carrying on, all hidden behind the small rituals of daily life.

The days passed in the quiet rhythm of the village, but something had shifted in Lakshmi's home since that day with the indigo saree. It was as if the fabric had pulled a thread in the heart of both mother and daughter, binding them closer in a way neither had expected. Nila began visiting more frequently, her gaze softer, her laughter mingling with her mother's as they shared meals and stories in the shaded veranda, while the salty breeze drifted in from the sea.

Lakshmi could feel her mother's presence more vividly now, as if the saree she kept folded on the upper shelf in her closet held fragments of Amma's voice, her warmth, her laughter. On special evenings, Lakshmi would bring it down, drape it over herself, and stroll out to the small garden where she'd once seen her mother tend to jasmine bushes. There, among the buds and blossoms, she would feel the weight of the past ease away, replaced by a lightness she couldn't explain.

One evening, Nila arrived as Lakshmi was lighting the evening lamp in front of the family's brass deity, her hands moving in practiced reverence. Nila watched her mother's form bathed in the soft glow of the vilakku, the indigo of the saree catching the light, casting a serene aura around her. Lakshmi looked up, surprised to see Nila lingering by the door.

"Ah, you're here early today," Lakshmi said, her face lighting up as she welcomed her daughter.

Nila approached slowly, her eyes on the saree. "Amma, you wear this saree so often now. I haven't seen you with anything else."

Lakshmi smiled, patting the edge of the fabric on her shoulder. "It brings me comfort, Nila. It reminds me of things I used to know, things I'd long forgotten. Sometimes," she said, her voice softening, "I feel Amma is with me, guiding me through the little things in life, as she always did."

Nila felt a pang in her chest, hearing her mother speak of such intangible things, things she'd never considered. She'd always seen Lakshmi as steady, practical, someone

who kept everything running smoothly, never one to dwell in memories or the past. This was a different woman, a woman she was only now getting to know.

The next morning, when Nila returned, she found Lakshmi sitting by the window, gazing at the shimmering horizon with a distant look in her eyes.

"Amma," Nila ventured gently, settling beside her. "Tell me about Paati. I only remember her cooking in the kitchen and fussing over my hair when I was little. But I feel like there's more I didn't see."

Lakshmi's face softened, her hands resting in her lap as memories filled her mind, memories she hadn't spoken of in years.

"Your Paati was the heart of this family," Lakshmi began, her voice steady and rich with emotion. "She wasn't educated in the way people are today, but she had a wisdom no school could teach. She knew each plant in our garden by its leaves, could tell when rain was coming just by the feel of the wind, and could calm any child with a story. She was a pillar, Nila. We all leaned on her, trusted her to be there no matter what."

Nila listened intently, feeling a sense of wonder and reverence for this woman she'd known only as a frail old grandmother. Her mind filled with images of her Paati in younger years, vibrant and strong, a woman who had lived a life full of spirit and resilience. She reached for her mother's hand, intertwining her fingers, feeling a warmth that radiated from this shared memory.

Lakshmi sighed, looking down at their hands. "I used to think I was nothing like her. Amma had this strength that seemed effortless. I struggled more—life was different for me, and I didn't have the same wisdom she did, or so I thought. But now, I feel her with me, showing me that maybe I carry her within me more than I realized."

In the days that followed, Nila found herself seeing her mother differently. Lakshmi's hands, which had always been busied with chores, now seemed to hold a quiet grace, a connection to something larger. She noticed the way her mother moved, the way she spoke, and how her laughter sounded so much like the stories of Paati she now treasured.

One morning, as they sat together over cups of hot, frothy coffee, Lakshmi glanced at her daughter with a tender smile.

"Nila, you're growing up so much," she said. "You remind me of myself when I was your age, and sometimes of Amma too. She taught me so much, things

I never thought I'd need, things I took for granted." She paused, a wistful look in her eyes. "I've been so caught up in my own ways, in what I had to do. But Amma taught me that caring is never just about doing—it's about being there, listening, knowing without words."

The words settled in the air, and Nila felt a weight in her heart, an awakening to her own mother's depth and the love that had always been there, unspoken but strong. She realized how Lakshmi had poured herself into her family, carrying on a legacy she hadn't fully understood until now.

Later that week, Lakshmi and Nila were in the market together, a rare outing that felt almost festive. They moved through the crowd, Lakshmi pointing out vendors she'd known for years, the ones who remembered her mother as well. As they passed a small stall selling handmade bangles, Nila stopped, her eyes falling on a delicate gold bangle with small etched patterns—a design that she remembered Paati wearing.

Without a word, she picked up the bangle and turned to her mother. "Amma, let's get this. It looks just like the ones Paati wore."

Lakshmi's eyes glistened with surprise and gratitude, and for a moment, it was as if they were both children under her mother's wing, gathering remnants of her spirit, piece by piece. She let Nila buy the bangle, slipping it onto her wrist, feeling its gentle weight and warmth.

As they made their way back home, the sun began to set, casting a soft glow over the village. The air was filled with the scent of the sea, mingling with the fragrance of the jasmine flowers blooming along their path. They walked in silence, their steps in sync, a comfortable, familiar rhythm between them.

When they arrived home, Lakshmi touched the edge of her saree, her fingers brushing over the zari border, as if drawing strength from it. She looked at Nila, who was watching her intently, with a look of deep affection and newfound respect.

"You know, Nila," she said softly, "we may grow older, move on, but some things stay with us, woven into who we are. Amma used to say that our loved ones live on in the things they've touched, in the memories they've left us. I feel that now, in every thread of this saree, in every corner of this home."

Nila nodded, her heart brimming with gratitude and love. In that moment, she understood that this connection to her mother, to her grandmother, was an inheritance richer than any material wealth, a legacy of love, strength, and unbroken ties. She realized that Lakshmi, too, was carrying this legacy forward, passing it down, one day, to her own children.

As dusk settled, they sat together, side by side, Lakshmi's bangle glinting softly in the fading light, the indigo saree flowing like a river of memories around her, enveloping them both in its embrace. The village outside quieted, and in the silence, Lakshmi and Nila sat, feeling the presence of Amma—her spirit woven into the fabric of their lives, as steadfast as the sea itself.

In the days that followed, Nila found herself visiting her mother more frequently, slipping into a rhythm that seemed as natural as breathing. She would arrive in the early morning or linger past sunset, helping Lakshmi with the housework, listening to her stories, and learning the recipes Lakshmi had once learned from her mother. Each visit felt like piecing together fragments of the past, as if she were weaving a new bond with her mother while reconnecting with her grandmother's memory.

One evening, a gentle rain drizzled over Periya Vaikal, creating tiny rivulets in the village lanes and adding a cool freshness to the air. Lakshmi sat by the window, wrapped in her indigo saree, the one that had now become almost like a second skin. Her fingers toyed with the bangle Nila had given her, and she found herself murmuring a prayer, an offering to her mother's memory.

Nila arrived later than usual that evening, her hair damp from the rain, carrying a small package under her arm. She entered the house with a quiet sense of purpose, her eyes warm and reflective.

"Amma," she called softly, settling down beside Lakshmi. "I brought something for you."

Lakshmi raised her eyebrows, intrigued, as Nila placed the package on her lap and urged her to open it. With careful fingers, Lakshmi unwrapped the cloth, revealing a beautifully woven sari in a deep, rich red. It was similar to her own indigo sari, with a delicate border and intricate zari work that glinted softly in the lamplight.

"Red," Lakshmi murmured, her voice choked with surprise and emotion. "I haven't worn this colour in years... not since Appa passed." She traced the edge of the sari, memories flooding her mind.

"I know, Amma," Nila said, her voice gentle. "But this isn't about anyone else. It's about you. This sari reminded me of the strength you carry, like Paati's strength. I thought... maybe you'd like to wear it, even just once."

Lakshmi stared at her daughter, feeling her heart swell with a mix of pride, love, and gratitude. She had worn only muted colours after her husband's passing, respecting tradition, but today she felt an unexpected pull—a desire to reclaim a part of herself that had been buried under years of routine and restraint.

That night, with Nila's help, Lakshmi draped herself in the red sari, feeling the weight and warmth of it settle over her shoulders. As she adjusted the pleats and draped the end gracefully over her shoulder, she saw a spark in her reflection that reminded her of her younger self, a woman of quiet strength and pride, much like her mother had been. Nila watched with an admiration that left her almost breathless; she felt as though she were seeing her mother for the first time, radiant, resplendent, timeless.

As the rain let up and the clouds parted, a sliver of moonlight slipped into the room, casting a soft glow around them both. They went outside, stepping into the small garden that had once been Amma's sanctuary.

The jasmine vines were heavy with blossoms, filling the air with their gentle, intoxicating fragrance. Lakshmi felt her heart lighten, as if her mother's spirit were there, guiding her, encouraging her.

Standing under the open sky, Lakshmi looked at her daughter and spoke words that felt like they had been waiting within her for years.

"Nila, I think… I think it's time I live a little more freely, as Amma would have wanted me to. I spent so much of my life trying to be as wise, as strong as she was, that I forgot to live for myself." She paused, her voice trembling slightly. "I don't want you to make the same mistake. Remember, we don't just carry the weight of those we love. We also carry their light."

Nila nodded, feeling a deep shift within herself, a realization that her mother's wisdom was as boundless as the sea before them. In that moment, she saw that her mother was not only the patient caregiver she had always known but also a woman who had dreams, desires, and an inner strength that went beyond her understanding.

With a smile, Nila took her mother's hand, feeling the pulse of something ancient and enduring passing between them—a promise, a legacy. She thought of her own children, her role as a mother, and felt a new sense of purpose and gratitude.

"Amma," she said softly, "I see Paati in you. I see her strength and her love, and I see you in me. This bond… it's what holds us all together. Thank you, for everything."

Lakshmi wrapped her arms around Nila, holding her close. In the silent embrace, they felt a wholeness, a connection that didn't need words to define it. Lakshmi understood that this was the legacy her mother had passed on, not through possessions or wealth, but through the quiet, enduring love that bound their family.

As they returned to the house, Lakshmi felt a lightness she hadn't felt in years. She wore the red sari that night, not as a break from tradition but as an act of self-honouring, of acknowledging the woman her mother had raised her to be. She was a daughter, a mother, and perhaps someday would become a grandmother, carrying forward the wisdom and love that had been passed down through generations.

In the days that followed, the village noticed a change in Lakshmi. She moved with a newfound grace, her steps lighter, her laughter richer. She wore her indigo sari on some days and her new red sari on others, each colour a tribute to the lives and memories woven into her heart. Her neighbours spoke of the dignity and joy that radiated from her, a beauty that only deepened with time.

For Nila, the moments she shared with her mother became cherished memories, a source of strength and guidance she would carry into her own journey as a mother. And for Lakshmi, these moments with her daughter were a reminder of her own mother's legacy— a legacy of love, resilience, and the quiet grace that held them all together.

As the seasons turned and the years rolled on, Lakshmi's story became a part of the village's lore—a story of a woman who wore her mother's love like a precious garment, and who, in the twilight of her life, found herself reborn in the colours of memory, love, and self-acceptance.

The Scooter Ride

In the quiet corner of Bengaluru's Jayanagar, where the trees still rustled with the nostalgic murmurs of old Bangalore, lived Ramanujam. A relic in his own right, he spent his days perched on the same wooden armchair by the window, watching the world shuffle past with mechanical regularity. Time had peeled away his once-bold spirit, leaving behind a quiet man whose dreams and memories only floated within the small confines of his modest home.

Ramanujam was once a rider. Not just any rider, mind you, but a daredevil, a rider of such repute that even in the chaos of Bangalore's narrow lanes, he would weave his motorbike through with the agility of a panther. In those days, he was known as "Jambu"—a name he'd earned because he was big-hearted, like the great jambu tree that stands unwavering and strong, providing shade to everyone beneath it. Back in his twenties, Jambu's bike had been his prized possession. It had a name, too—"Black Bullet." No one could say where Jambu ended and the Bullet began. They were, after all, a single entity blazing through life's twists and turns.

As time and age had their say, the Black Bullet had found itself a place in a dusty corner of Ramanujam's small shed. His eyesight dimmed, his bones creaked, and Bengaluru's traffic bloomed into an unstoppable cacophony. The once-lithe Jambu now hesitated to cross even the busy lanes of Jayanagar on his own.

Ramanujam's granddaughter, Priya, knew only fragments of her Thatha's youth. She had heard enough stories from her mother about the legendary Jambu to look upon the old man with admiration, mingled with faint disbelief. After all, this quiet, slightly stooped figure who waited for his morning filter coffee and shuffled about the house didn't quite match the image of a dashing biker who had once painted the town red.

One weekend, after noticing her grandfather's reluctance to step outside even for a walk in the nearby park, Priya had an idea.

"Thatha," she began one Saturday morning, "how about we go out for a ride today?"

Ramanujam raised an eyebrow, an expression he had all but forgotten to use. His voice, gravelly but gentle, replied, "Where will we go, Priya? And how will we go?"

"On my scooter!" Priya's face lit up with a mischievous gleam. She knew her suggestion was a little unorthodox. "Come, it'll be fun. I'll show you around all your old haunts. You used to ride a bike; you'll be at home on a scooter."

Ramanujam was silent for a long time. A scooter ride. He hadn't been on any two-wheeler for years now. It was, after all, an unsightly affair for an old man to be hanging onto a scooter, zipping past with a young girl at the helm. But Priya's face, full of hope and affection, melted something inside him.

"You…you want to take an old man like me out?" Ramanujam's voice cracked slightly, and he looked away, feeling almost embarrassed at his own vulnerability.

"Of course, Thatha!" Priya exclaimed, "I'll even let you pick the route."

And so, a little after breakfast, Ramanujam found himself wearing his old jacket. He chuckled to himself, wondering if it still fit him the way it used to. He didn't have a helmet, but Priya had thought of everything. She held out a brand-new one, a bright blue with a small sticker of Lord Hanuman on the side.

"For strength," she said with a grin.

Ramanujam nodded solemnly, putting the helmet on, feeling the weight of memories, it awakened. With Priya leading him to the scooter, he awkwardly climbed on, holding the edges of the seat gingerly, almost afraid it might tip over. But when Priya started the engine, a familiar purr beneath him stirred something deeper within. The cityscape stretched before him like an old friend, and as the scooter pulled out of the driveway, he felt a bit of his younger self nudging awake.

Their first stop was Lalbagh. As they wound through Bengaluru's chaotic streets, Ramanujam took in the world around him with a new intensity. So much had changed. He had always thought the city would remember him as he remembered it. But the wide roads and sprawling buildings were like strangers in a place he once knew as intimately as his own hand.

When they reached Lalbagh, Priya parked and turned to him, watching him take in the sights. He looked at the grand trees with their sprawling roots, the small vendors hawking their jasmine garlands, and the large banyan under which he used to meet his friends.

"Did you know, Priya," he began, "we used to come here every Sunday morning, five or six of us. We'd ride in a line, like some great procession, and end here at Lalbagh. We'd spend hours just talking and laughing."

Priya looked at him, a soft smile on her face. "Why did you stop coming, Thatha?"

Ramanujam looked away, hesitant. "Ah, child, life changes. Work gets in the way, friends drift apart, new buildings come up where once there was open space. The city and I, we grew older together, but not in the same direction."

After a few moments of silence, Priya nodded toward the scooter. "Ready for the next spot?"

Ramanujam grinned. "Take me to the bridge over Koramangala Lake, if it's still there!"

They zipped through the streets, the wind a pleasant balm against the coolness of the morning. Ramanujam held on, his eyes bright, as they maneuverer past the various landmarks. Soon, they were at the old bridge over Koramangala Lake. It was hardly recognizable. A new steel railing had replaced the old wooden one, and the small park by the lake had turned into a complex of shops and high-rises.

"Here?" Priya asked, looking around.

"Yes. Here," he said softly. He closed his eyes, recalling the lake as it once was—a serene expanse of water, dotted with lotuses and kingfishers. In the evenings, the sun would cast a golden hue over it, making it look like a shimmering blanket of light. He and his friend Vasu would stop here, taking a break from their rides to gaze at the reflection of the sky in the water. It had always felt like their own secret spot.

As he opened his eyes, the lake, now smaller and shrouded by the shadows of the high-rise buildings, looked tired, a bit like him. But a strange sense of peace filled him. Just being here, with Priya's laughter filling the air around him, he could almost feel the presence of his old friend by his side.

"Thatha, what's so funny?" Priya asked, noticing his smile.

"Oh, just an old memory. Vasu and I, we used to come here…we'd talk about all the grand plans we had. It was silly, really." He chuckled softly. "Vasu used to say he'd own half the city one day. And here we are. The city is owned by strangers, and Vasu is in Canada, chasing some other dream."

Priya reached over and placed her hand gently on his arm. "I'm glad you came out today, Thatha."

Ramanujam turned to her, the corners of his eyes crinkling in a smile. "You know, Priya, I'm glad too. It's been years since I felt the wind on my face like this. You brought me back to myself, in a way."

They spent a few more minutes on the bridge before heading off toward their final stop: Ramanujam's old neighbourhood in Malleswaram. As they turned down the familiar streets, a strange pang of nostalgia hit him. The houses were newer, the people different, but the spirit of Malleswaram lingered like the faint aroma of jasmine in the air.

When they finally arrived, Ramanujam pointed out the house he had grown up in—a simple two-story building, now painted a faded yellow, with a large mango tree standing sentinel outside.

"Here," he whispered, almost to himself. "Here is where it all began."

Priya parked the scooter and followed him as he walked slowly toward the house, his gaze lingering on every detail. A small boy, no older than ten, was playing in the front yard with a cricket bat. When he noticed Ramanujam, he paused and looked up.

"Hello, uncle!" the boy called out with a toothy grin.

Ramanujam smiled, a small wave of warmth coursing through him. "Hello, little one," he replied, giving a gentle wave.

It was in that moment that Ramanujam realized something. The city might have changed, the people might have moved on, and his own youth may have become a shadow of memory. But his spirit, that old daredevil who had once ridden a motorbike with abandon, still lingered. And for the first time in years, he felt as though he, too, belonged here.

As they rode back, the sun began its slow descent, casting a soft orange glow over the city. The world felt lighter, and with his heart swelling in gratitude, Ramanujam leaned forward and whispered, "Thank you, Priya. You brought me back home."

Priya glanced back with a smile that seemed to say, Welcome back, Thatha.

The weeks after Ramanujam's scooter ride with Priya were filled with an unusual liveliness in the household.

Each morning, Priya would find her Thatha whistling as he read the paper, or lingering by the window, watching the street below with a spark in his eye. It was as if the ride had unlocked something deep within him—a glimmer of the old Jambu had returned.

One Saturday morning, as Priya prepared tea in the kitchen, she heard a hesitant clearing of the throat behind her.

"Priya," Ramanujam began, his voice carrying a tinge of mischief, "I was wondering if you'd like to take your old Thatha on another ride. This time, I have a special place in mind."

Priya turned, surprised and amused, watching as Ramanujam shifted his weight from foot to foot like an excited child. "Of course, Thatha! But only if you tell me where we're going."

Ramanujam chuckled, a low rumble that made Priya smile. "Ah, but that would spoil the fun. I'll give you a clue, though. It's a place that has barely changed in fifty years."

An hour later, with Priya at the helm and Ramanujam clutching her shoulders, they set off through the winding streets of Jayanagar. Ramanujam's instructions were cryptic, directing her around twists and turns, finally leading them to a part of Bengaluru he hadn't visited in years.

They arrived at an old café, tucked away behind a row of fragrant jasmine vendors and paan shops. The faded sign read, "Shanti Tea House." The place looked unremarkable from the outside—its paint was peeling, the awning was torn, and the small windows were covered with a thin film of dust. But the sight of it filled Ramanujam's heart with a quiet thrill.

"Here?" Priya asked, looking at the old, nondescript building with curiosity.

"Ah, yes," Ramanujam said, his eyes twinkling. "This place holds memories you wouldn't believe, child. In my youth, this was the only place in town where you could get filter coffee that rivalled what Amma made. It was our gathering spot, my friends and I. We'd talk, argue, and laugh until our sides ached."

They stepped inside, greeted by the comforting aroma of freshly brewed coffee mingling with the smell of old wood. The café was nearly empty except for a couple of elderly men sitting in one corner, sipping tea and reading newspapers. The walls were lined with old black-and-white photographs of Bengaluru—pictures of the old Majestic Theatre, Russell Market, and the grand Mysore Bank building. Ramanujam's eyes lingered on each photograph, each one evoking an era he remembered with bittersweet fondness.

As they took their seats, a waiter with greying hair and a warm smile approached them.

"Ramanujam sir! Is it really you?" the waiter exclaimed, astonishment lighting up his face.

Ramanujam chuckled, waving his hand dismissively. "Yes, Shankar, it's me. Still alive, as you can see!"

Shankar beamed, clapping his hands together. "It's been so long, sir! I thought you had moved away like everyone else."

Ramanujam introduced Priya to Shankar, who quickly disappeared to prepare "special coffee" for his old patron. The drinks arrived in tall, brass tumblers, the aroma evoking memories as vivid as the present. Ramanujam held the warm tumbler in his hands, savouring the comfort it brought.

Priya watched her grandfather sip his coffee, an odd stillness in his demeanour. She had always known Ramanujam as the gentle elder of the house, but today, as she observed his quiet intensity, she glimpsed another layer—a man who had known the pulse of the city, who had walked its streets with purpose.

"Thatha," she began, breaking the comfortable silence. "Did you ever dream of leaving Bengaluru?"

Ramanujam looked up, the question taking him by surprise. "I did, once. There was a time when I thought of moving abroad, perhaps to London or even America. The thought of adventure thrilled me."

He paused, his eyes distant. "But then, I realized that no matter where I went, Bengaluru was where my heart truly belonged. This city… it has its quirks, its faults, but it's woven into my very being. Leaving it would be like leaving a part of myself behind."

Priya listened, feeling a newfound respect for her grandfather. "Thatha, tell me more about the Bengaluru you knew."

Ramanujam's eyes lit up, and he leaned forward, resting his elbows on the table as he spoke. "Ah, where do I begin? This city was once a place of serenity. We didn't have these tall buildings casting shadows everywhere. It was all low roofs, gulmohar trees in bloom, and lakes so vast you'd think they were oceans. There was a magic to the air—a slower pace that allowed us to breathe and truly live."

He told her about the annual flower shows at Lalbagh, the bustling bazaars in Chickpet where he'd buy sandalwood for his mother, and the occasional escapades to Cubbon Park with his friends, where they would spend hours on the sprawling lawns, planning futures they could barely imagine.

"And then there were the theatres!" Ramanujam said with a glint of excitement. "The grand Majestic Theatre, the smaller ones along Kempegowda Road. In those days, going to the movies was an event. We'd dress up, gather our friends, and queue outside hours in advance. We'd watch Rajkumar and MGR with awe, cheering and whistling like children."

Priya smiled as he painted a picture of a world she could only imagine—a simpler, more intimate Bengaluru that seemed as mythical as a story from a book.

As they finished their coffee, Priya noticed that the elderly men in the corner had begun watching Ramanujam with mild curiosity. One of them, a man with a frail frame but bright eyes, rose from his seat and approached their table.

"Ramanujam, isn't it?" the man asked hesitantly, a hint of nostalgia in his voice.

Ramanujam looked up, squinting before recognition dawned on his face. "Ravi! My goodness, it's been years!"

They shook hands, the kind of handshake that speaks of long-forgotten camaraderie. Ravi pulled up a chair, and the two men began reminiscing about old friends and shared memories, their voices filling the small café with laughter and warmth. Priya watched them with fascination, witnessing a part of her grandfather's life she had never known.

"Do you remember that one Diwali?" Ravi said, a twinkle in his eye. "The one when we dared each other to set off rockets on that narrow lane in Malleswaram? The constable chased us for half an hour!"

Ramanujam laughed heartily, nodding. "Yes, and we all hid behind Vasu's house, only to find out he was hiding with his mother in the kitchen, pretending to study!"

The two old friends dissolved into laughter, their shared memories peeling away the years. Priya couldn't help but feel a pang of emotion. This wasn't just her Thatha; this was a man with a life full of friends, adventures, and stories that stretched far beyond her understanding.

As they prepared to leave, Shankar came over, refusing to let them pay. "This one is on me, Ramanujam sir. It's a joy to see you here again."

Ramanujam nodded graciously, patting Shankar's shoulder. "Thank you, Shankar. It's good to be here."

Back on the scooter, as they wound through the streets, Ramanujam fell silent. The café visit had stirred memories long buried, of friendships and places that had slipped into the past. But he also felt a renewed strength, a sense of pride in having lived those moments so fully.

"Thatha," Priya said gently as they approached home. "I didn't realize how much this city meant to you."

Ramanujam looked at her, his expression softening. "It's not just the city, Priya. It's the life I've lived here. It's the people, the friendships, the laughter, and yes, even the heartache. This city has grown, changed, even forgotten people like me. But I still carry it all here." He placed his hand over his heart.

Priya nodded, understanding more than she could express. "Thatha," she ventured, "maybe next weekend, we could take the scooter out again. There must be so many places left for you to show me."

Ramanujam smiled, his eyes twinkling with a renewed zest. "Ah, there are places, child, many places. But I think next time, I'll be the one steering."

Priya's laugh echoed down the street, and as they pulled into the driveway, Ramanujam felt that familiar purr of the scooter beneath him, awakening not just memories but a spirit he had almost forgotten.

The next weekend arrived with a crisp, clear sky over Bengaluru, the kind that hinted at gentle warmth and just the right breeze. Ramanujam was already awake, bustling with an energy that amused the rest of the family. He had decided that today was the day he would take charge of the scooter, just like in the days of his youth. Though his family expressed some concern, they couldn't deny the spark in his eyes—a glimmer that seemed to erase years from his face.

"Thatha," Priya said as she held out the scooter keys, "are you sure you're ready for this?"

Ramanujam gave her a playful scoff, grabbing the keys with a mock flourish. "I'm as ready as I was at twenty-five. Watch, and you'll see that the old Jambu still remembers a thing or two."

With a bit of help from Priya, Ramanujam climbed onto the scooter, adjusting himself with great deliberation. Priya took her seat behind him, her arms firmly around his waist. She felt a strange thrill, a mix of excitement and nervousness, as her grandfather started the scooter with a confidence that belied his years.

As they eased out of the driveway, Ramanujam's hands settled comfortably on the handles, and he took a slow, practiced breath. The hum of the engine felt like a familiar song, one he hadn't sung in years. They cruised down the streets of Jayanagar, Priya watching the neighbours peering curiously at the unusual sight of the elderly Ramanujam riding a scooter with his young granddaughter in tow.

Their first stop was a small, unassuming temple nestled in a quiet alleyway. Ramanujam parked the scooter and led Priya up the narrow stone steps. Inside, the temple was tranquil, with only a few oil lamps flickering near the deity. Priya watched as her grandfather folded his hands, bowing his head reverently. She followed suit, feeling the peace of the temple settle over her.

"This temple," Ramanujam began, his voice barely above a whisper, "was where I came before any big decision. It's seen my hopes, my worries, and my promises. When I bought my first bike, I came here to ask for protection. And when I married your grandmother, this was the first place we came together as husband and wife."

Priya felt a lump form in her throat. She could sense the reverence in his voice, the unspoken emotions that lingered between the words.

As they left the temple, Priya noticed a serene smile on her Thatha's face, a peace she hadn't seen before. She felt as if they had stepped into a part of his life, one she had never known and would now carry with her.

They continued their journey, weaving through narrow lanes until they reached Cubbon Park. Ramanujam parked the scooter under a sprawling banyan tree, and they strolled along the sun-dappled path. They found a bench under a gulmohar tree, its red blossoms bright against the green of the park.

"I used to come here often," Ramanujam said, his voice tinged with nostalgia. "In those days, Cubbon Park felt like a whole world in itself. We'd come here, me and my friends, after a long day of work. We'd sit, sometimes talking, sometimes just watching the world pass by."

"Did you have a best friend, Thatha?" Priya asked, glancing at him curiously.

Ramanujam looked away, his gaze distant, as if sifting through a chest of old memories. "Yes, Vasu was my closest friend. We were like brothers. Inseparable, as they say. He was the one who gave me the nickname 'Jambu' because, in his words, I had a heart as big as the jambu tree."

Priya watched him, sensing the wistfulness in his voice. "Where is he now?"

Ramanujam sighed. "Life took us in different directions. He went abroad, and we slowly lost touch. I hear he's still in Canada. But I haven't spoken to him in years."

A comfortable silence fell between them as they watched children playing nearby and the occasional elderly couple strolling by. For the first time, Priya understood how much her grandfather had given to this city, his friendships, and his memories—all woven into the fabric of Bengaluru.

After a while, Ramanujam rose, dusting off his trousers. "Come, child," he said, a twinkle in his eye. "There's one last place I want to show you."

They got back on the scooter, and he directed her to a quiet neighbourhood on the edge of Malleswaram. Here, the streets were lined with old bungalows, the kind with wide verandas and sloping roofs. They stopped in front of a small, weathered house, its paint faded and a mango tree standing proudly in the front yard.

"This," he said softly, "was my first home after marriage. Your grandmother and I spent the first years of our life together here."

Priya could see the emotion in his eyes, the bittersweet memories that flooded back. She imagined a younger

Ramanujam, his wife by his side, laughing and dreaming under the very mango tree that stood before them.

"You know," Ramanujam said, his voice tinged with sadness, "your grandmother had a swing right here, under this tree. She'd spend hours reading, or simply watching the street, always humming a tune. She had a way of making everything feel like home."

Priya squeezed his hand, feeling his grief and love intertwine. She had never known her grandmother, who had passed away when she was very young, but hearing her Thatha speak of her, she felt an inexplicable closeness to the woman who had once graced his life. Ramanujam took a deep breath, letting the memories settle. After a moment, he turned to Priya, his eyes glistening with a warmth that belied his age.

"Thank you, Priya," he said, his voice steady but full of emotion. "Thank you for giving me this gift, for letting me relive these places and moments."

Priya hugged him, her heart brimming with love and respect. "No, Thatha, thank you for sharing all this with me. I understand you better now, and I feel like I know my roots, my family, in a way I never did before." They rode home in a comfortable silence, the golden evening light casting long shadows over the streets. When they pulled into the driveway, Ramanujam sat on the scooter for a moment, as if reluctant to let the day end.

As Priya helped him off, he looked at her with a gentle smile. "You know, Priya," he said, his voice soft, "this city may change, people may move on, but these moments we've had—they'll stay with me. And one day, I hope they stay with you too."

Priya nodded, feeling a deep sense of gratitude. She knew that the city, the memories, and her grandfather's stories had left an indelible mark on her. She had glimpsed a world that was rich with laughter, friendship, and love—a world that her Thatha had built with every street, every tree, and every memory he had cherished.

That night, as Ramanujam sat in his armchair by the window, watching the soft glow of the streetlights outside, he felt a profound sense of peace. The old Jambu had taken one last ride, rediscovered his city, and found a new connection with his granddaughter. And for the first time in years, he felt truly, wonderfully alive.

The Banyan Tree Meetings

In the heart of the small Tamil Nadu village of Thottakudi stood a sprawling banyan tree, its roots winding deep into the earth and its branches reaching skyward like ancient arms cradling the heavens. It was a tree that everyone knew, a tree that even the youngest child in the village referred to as "thatha maram"—Grandfather Tree. Under its cool shade, men of age and wisdom gathered each morning as the first light touched the dusty streets, and the birds began their song.

The banyan tree was not just a tree. It was a silent witness, an old friend to the villagers, a place where men in their twilight years convened, their white dhotis fluttering in the breeze, their voices murmuring, and their laughter rising like incense. They called these gatherings "The Banyan Tree Meetings," and the village knew them as sacred, unchanging, and somehow essential to the day's rhythm.

Each man who came here had his own reason. There was Ramasamy, a retired schoolmaster with a voice that could command any child's obedience in a second. He sat cross-legged on a low stone under the banyan's shade, his spectacles perched on his nose, looking around with an air of someone who had seen much, judged much, and remained serenely wise. Then there was Paati Kuppuswamy, who once owned the only flour mill in the village, his hands thick and calloused from decades of grinding grain. He still wore the miller's dusty towel around his neck, as if even in retirement he feared he might need to lift a heavy sack at a moment's notice. A little apart from him sat Balakrishnan, who had once travelled as far as Mumbai, and liked to remind everyone of it as often as possible. And always at the fringes was young Gopal, no more than forty, an oddity among these men who had mostly seen sixty summers. He had lost his father early, and somehow found comfort in these conversations, treating the elders like his own family.

On this morning, a gentle breeze stirred the leaves, and the sun filtered down in shifting patterns. The men sat in their usual circle, speaking of family, of the monsoon rains that seemed delayed this year, and of how Ramasamy's youngest grandson was finding city life difficult in Chennai. Their topics were familiar, yet every day they found new things to say. It was as if they were not merely chatting, but weaving together strands of memory, holding each other's lives in reverent hands, sharing the load of their journeys.

It was during one such exchange that the first hints of trouble arrived, though the men took it lightly. Young Siva, who worked as a clerk in the town office, ran up, slightly out of breath. "Ayya, have you heard? They say they will clear this whole area for the new road. The Collector wants to build a better road straight from Thottakudi to the main highway."

Balakrishnan, who had once taken a train to Mumbai and fancied himself an expert on modern life, chuckled, "Ah, so they are bringing the city to us now! Soon we will all have automobiles flying down our streets, and we will have to wait to cross our own lanes!"

The others laughed, waving their hands dismissively. But Ramasamy's eyes narrowed behind his thick spectacles. "It may be true," he said. "And if it is, we will not be able to stop it. This banyan tree has been here long before us, and it will likely live longer. But if it stands in the way of a government road…"

The air grew tense. The men exchanged looks, unease creeping into their familiar meeting place. They had seen the village change over the years, watched new houses come up, seen the rice fields shrink. But the banyan tree had remained constant. It was as if the tree had promised to be there for as long as they needed it. They could not imagine life without it, nor could they imagine these gatherings in any other place.

Several days passed, and the meetings continued under the banyan tree, with its roots entwined in the men's memories, standing as a reminder of things larger than human plans. Then one morning, the Collector arrived. He was a young man, straight-backed and newly posted to the region, carrying with him an air of authority and city-slick efficiency. He strolled into the village flanked by two assistants and a surveyor, his crisp white shirt and perfectly pleated pants making him look almost too shiny, too polished, in the dusty, earthy atmosphere of Thottakudi.

The men watched him approach, curiosity mingling with a slow-growing resentment. The Collector stood before them, clearing his throat in a manner that suggested he expected a respectful silence. Ramasamy glanced at his companions, a look passing between them that said, "Let him speak, but we are no schoolboys waiting for a lesson."

"Good morning, gentlemen," the Collector began, his voice smooth and formal. "As you may have heard, we are planning to extend the road through your village. This will be a great benefit for all of you, especially for the younger generations. A proper road will mean faster transport, better access to hospitals, schools, and markets. The government has approved this project to modernize the area."

There was a murmur of mild agreement from a few of the younger villagers who had gathered nearby. But the old men remained silent, watching him with steady, unyielding eyes. The Collector went on, "Unfortunately, this means that we will need to clear some land. And, regrettably, this includes your banyan tree."

The silence deepened, became something heavy and immovable. The men sat as still as the tree itself, a quiet strength gathering among them. Finally, Ramasamy stood up, his lean frame taut, his eyes sharp behind his spectacles. "Collector Sir," he said slowly, his voice carrying both courtesy and defiance, "this banyan tree is not merely a tree to us. It is part of our lives, a place where we gather, where we remember those who came before us. My father sat under this tree, and his father before him. It is our meeting ground, our council, our shelter."

The Collector's face remained composed, but his tone turned faintly patronizing. "I understand, sir, that this tree holds sentimental value. But you must also understand that progress sometimes requires sacrifice. We must think of the future, of the greater good."

Balakrishnan, who until then had been listening quietly, sprang up, his voice rising with indignation. "Progress? Who says this road will be good for us? You city people come here, deciding what is best for us, without asking if we want it. Do we not already have enough good things here? A quiet life, family, friendship… this tree?"

The Collector seemed taken aback by the strength of the opposition, and the small crowd that had gathered around began murmuring in agreement. He looked at his assistants, who shuffled their feet, and back at the men, who stood like old warriors ready to defend their last stronghold. "I… I must follow orders," he said finally, his voice losing some of its confidence. "The decision is not mine alone. But I will… I will convey your concerns to my superiors."

With that, he turned and left, his assistants trailing behind him. The villagers watched him go, a strange feeling of triumph mingling with worry. They had won a skirmish, but they knew the battle was far from over.

For the next several days, the Banyan Tree Meetings became strategy sessions. The men discussed every possible way to save the tree, considering appeals to the village headman, letters to district officials, and even, if all else failed, chaining themselves to the banyan in protest. Young Gopal, whose respect for the elders had only grown, offered to help them write petitions and gather signatures. The village rallied, not just out of love for the tree, but out of respect for the old men and the life they had shared under its branches.

And so the banyan tree became a symbol. It was no longer just a place of rest but a testament to the soul of the village, a living history woven into the lives of its people. The Collector, faced with an unprecedented pushback from the community, began to reconsider his plans. But he, too, had orders from above, and he struggled with the decision as though he, too, felt some connection to the silent grandeur of the tree.

The men returned to their daily meetings, but now their conversations were different. They spoke less of the past and more of the future, not their own, but the future of the tree and the young ones who would one day sit under its shade. In their way, they knew they were fighting for something larger than any single memory or any one man's love for the old banyan. They were defending the spirit of their village, the roots of which ran just as deep as the roots of their beloved thatha maram.

The Banyan Tree Meetings, for these old men, had now become a battle for dignity, a stand against a world that changed too fast, a world that sometimes forgot to look back at what it might lose.

Word had spread across Thottakudi like a wind stirring dry leaves. The Collector's plan to uproot the banyan tree had ignited an unseen fire in the hearts of the villagers, young and old. Children whispered about it as they played, adults paused their work to exchange opinions, and even the women who came to fetch water from the village well spoke of it in hushed but firm tones. "Our men are standing up for that tree," they'd say with pride, a glint in their eyes, as though their husbands and fathers were warriors in some ancient, noble cause.

The village elders gathered under the banyan tree as usual, but now their quiet circle had grown. Younger men, women, and even a few children came to listen. The once tranquil banyan tree meetings were now vibrant, buzzing with plans and strategies. The place itself seemed alive, the breeze carrying whispers of resolve from one villager to another.

One evening, Ramasamy, the retired schoolmaster, stood up and addressed the crowd that had gathered under the banyan. "This tree is not just ours," he said, his voice steady and strong, "but it belongs to the land, to those who came before us and those who will come after. If they cut down this tree, they will sever the roots that connect us to our history. Are we going to let that happen?"

There was a murmur of agreement. Even young Gopal, who usually listened from the sidelines, felt a strange surge of pride in his heart, as if he were part of something far greater than himself. He looked around at the faces of the villagers, noticing the same feeling reflected in their eyes—a determination to preserve their way of life.

As night fell, a group of villagers approached the district office with a petition signed by nearly everyone in Thottakudi. The village's headman, who had once viewed the Collector's Road project as a mark of prestige, was now wavering, swayed by the collective will of his people. He had signed the petition, too, reluctantly but surely. They handed the petition to the Collector's assistant, a young man with a thin moustache who looked uncomfortable as he accepted the document. He nodded politely, but his eyes betrayed his unease, and he gave no promises.

Days turned into weeks, and the men continued their gatherings under the banyan tree. Yet a shadow hung over them. Each morning, they half-expected to see a line of government trucks waiting to uproot their tree. It was in this anxious time that Balakrishnan, who had become something of an unofficial spokesman, called for a special meeting.

"We must go to the Collector himself," he declared, his voice resolute. "We will tell him why this tree matters to us. Words on paper can be ignored, but our voices cannot."

And so, it was decided. A delegation of the village elders—Ramasamy, Balakrishnan, Kuppuswamy, and young Gopal—would go to the Collector's office. They dressed in their best white shirts and dhotis, a silent dignity radiating from their bearing as they walked, chins lifted, toward the town centre.

When they arrived at the Collector's office, they found themselves waiting in a dim corridor, flanked by chairs filled with officials and clerks busy with files and documents. It was a long wait, but the elders sat patiently, their faces calm. Only Gopal fidgeted, feeling slightly out of place among these men who carried themselves with an air of timeless authority.

Finally, the Collector appeared. He greeted them formally, his eyes moving swiftly from one face to another, landing last on Ramasamy, whose dignified posture seemed to command respect. Ramasamy spoke first, his words calm but unyielding.

"Collector sir," he said, "we come to you not as rebels, but as your people, the people of Thottakudi. We ask that you reconsider this decision to uproot our banyan tree. This tree is the soul of our village, a place where lives are shared, wisdom is passed on, and memories are held. If you take it away, you will cut away a piece of us."

The Collector listened, his expression unreadable, yet there was a hint of impatience in his posture. "I understand your sentiments, Ramasamy-ji, but as I have said before, progress sometimes requires sacrifice. The road will bring development and opportunities for the village. Imagine what it would mean for your children and grandchildren."

Balakrishnan, his hands trembling slightly but his voice steady, replied, "We have children, yes, and they will need opportunities. But they also need roots. This tree gives them that, a sense of who they are and where they come from. Can we not have both—a road and our tree?"

The Collector paused, glancing out of his window toward the town beyond. He seemed to be weighing his response. Finally, he sighed, leaning forward. "Gentlemen," he said softly, "your words move me, truly. I see that this tree is more than a tree to you. However, there are larger forces at play. I am but one man in a chain of command, following orders. I may appeal on your behalf, but I cannot promise more than that."

The elders exchanged looks, understanding that while they had been heard, they had not been assured. They left the office with heavy hearts, feeling as though they were fighting an invisible battle, their voices carried only as far as the echo of their footsteps.

Days passed, and the tension in the village mounted. The tree still stood, but its fate was uncertain. A strange quiet settled over the Banyan Tree Meetings. Even Balakrishnan, usually spirited and jovial, had grown subdued. The men sat in silence, each absorbed in his thoughts. But beneath the stillness lay a steely resolve, the unspoken understanding that if they were to lose the tree, they would not lose it quietly.

And then, one morning, the unthinkable happened. Just as the first light touched the village, the rumble of trucks echoed down the dirt path. The villagers rushed out of their homes, the elders already gathered under the banyan tree, their faces pale but their stance firm. The Collector arrived shortly after, flanked by his assistants and a crew of workers with saws and axes in hand. The sight of the old men standing there, silent but defiant, made the young official falter.

Ramasamy stepped forward. "Collector sir," he said, his voice barely a whisper but carrying a weight that stopped the workers in their tracks, "are you truly prepared to cut this tree, knowing what it means to us?"

The Collector hesitated, his face a mixture of discomfort and determination. "I… I have no choice," he replied, his voice sounding almost uncertain. "I must do my duty."

But the elders did not move. Kuppuswamy, who had rarely spoken during the meetings, suddenly raised his hand. "If you want to cut the tree," he said, his voice clear and unwavering, "you must go through us. We will not move."

One by one, the elders took their places around the banyan tree, standing in a circle, their arms stretched out, as though they were preparing to shield the tree with their very lives. Young Gopal, filled with a fierce pride, joined them, standing shoulder to shoulder with the men he had come to respect as family. The villagers gathered behind them, a silent wall of resolve, as if the tree had rooted them all together.

The Collector looked at them, the defiance in their eyes, the solidarity in their stance. He could not ignore them any longer. He felt the weight of his orders like a heavy stone, but he also felt something else—a strange respect for these men, who were prepared to sacrifice everything for a tree.

At that moment, something shifted in him. He turned to his workers, raising his hand to signal them to stop. There was a collective exhale among the villagers, a momentary pause as they waited, their hearts pounding.

The Collector approached Ramasamy, his face softening. "Perhaps," he said slowly, "there is another way. I will do what I can to preserve the tree, even if it means altering the road's path. This is not an easy request to fulfil, but your resolve has moved me. I will... I will speak to my superiors."

The elders' faces broke into quiet smiles. They knew they had won not just a reprieve for the tree but something even more valuable—a place for their voices in a world that often forgot them. The Collector departed, and as the trucks rumbled away, the village erupted in cheers.

That day, the banyan tree seemed to stand a little taller, its roots a little deeper, as though it too knew it had been saved. The elders resumed their meetings, their conversations now filled with stories of courage, of how one old tree had reminded the world of the dignity of age, the value of memory, and the quiet strength of community.

The days passed quietly after the villagers' stand against the Collector. The elders returned to their usual gatherings under the banyan tree, but their conversations felt lighter, their voices more vibrant, as if they had all aged backwards a little, filled with the Vigor of a small but meaningful victory. They no longer spoke much about the road. Instead, they recounted the old stories with fresh pride, stories that echoed through the branches, tales woven into the tree's roots like threads in a tapestry.

Ramasamy, the retired schoolmaster, took up his seat under the banyan one morning, gazing at the patchwork of sunlit leaves above. His usual group joined him in contented silence, settling into their familiar places like returning to a favourite home. The tree, with its ancient roots and sprawling branches, seemed somehow stronger, as if it too understood the village's loyalty. Even the children who played around it sensed something sacred, skirting its roots with new respect.

One afternoon, when the sun hung low in a pink-tinged sky, a jeep rolled into the village. The Collector had returned, though this time his air of formality was softened, and he walked toward the banyan tree without his usual entourage of assistants. His head bowed slightly, his demeanour as humble as any other villager. He found Ramasamy and the others seated as usual and greeted them with folded hands. "Ayya!," he began, "I bring news." The old men looked at each other, then back at the young official, their faces calm but attentive.

"I spoke with my superiors," the Collector continued. "They understand the importance of this tree and what it means to the village. They have agreed to spare it. The road will take a slight detour, preserving the banyan tree for all of you and your children."

A collective sigh of relief swept through the small gathering, a quiet but powerful wave of gratitude. Balakrishnan, the elder who had once travelled to Mumbai, slapped his knee with satisfaction. "Aha!" he exclaimed, "This tree's roots are too deep to be moved so easily!" The Collector smiled, seeming almost boyish in that moment. "It is true," he replied. "I underestimated its importance—and yours. Perhaps we who work in offices, chasing development, sometimes lose sight of what is truly valuable." He looked around at the villagers who had gathered, his gaze lingering on the banyan tree, where generations had come together for stories, wisdom, and companionship.

Ramasamy rose slowly, his joints creaking with age but his face glowing with a soft dignity. "Collector sir," he said, "we are grateful. But you must also know that we are not against development. We know change is necessary, that roads and schools and hospitals are the needs of tomorrow. But we also know that some things—the things that give us roots, that connect us to those before us—must be protected." The Collector nodded, his respect evident. "I understand, sir. Perhaps this banyan tree is a reminder that development can grow alongside tradition. This tree is not only yours—it is now a part of the spirit of Thottakudi itself."

As the news spread, the village buzzed with quiet joy. Even the younger generation, those who often found the elders' ways quaint and old-fashioned, felt a surge of pride. For the first time, they saw the banyan tree not just as part of the background, but as a symbol of resilience, of heritage that didn't wither with age. The tree had not only withstood the test of time but had now triumphed over the force of modernity itself, carving out a place for tradition alongside progress.

In the following days, something remarkable happened. The village children, who had always regarded the Banyan Tree Meetings as the business of the old, began to linger nearby, listening in on the elders' conversations. Young boys and girls sat cross-legged on the ground, wide-eyed as Ramasamy recounted tales of his youth, stories of bravery, and moments of foolishness he'd witnessed over the years. Even the teenagers, who often escaped to the nearby town, found themselves drawn to the banyan tree, seeking stories and guidance, as if a magnetic force pulled them to the heart of the village.

The banyan tree had once been a place for the elderly, but now it became a place for the entire village, a living bridge between generations. Gopal, the youngest among the elders, began organizing small events under the tree—festivals celebrating harvests, story nights, and even local talent shows. The banyan tree became a centre of community life, a place where everyone, young and old, felt a sense of belonging.

Years passed, and change came as it inevitably does. The road was built, hospitals and schools sprang up nearby, and some villagers moved to the city, lured by the promise of a different life. Yet the banyan tree remained, a steady guardian of the village's memory. The meetings under its shade continued, each elder passing down stories to new generations, as their faces aged and changed, and as children grew into adults who brought their own children to sit beneath the old branches.

One day, Ramasamy—now very old, his body frail but his spirit as lively as ever—sat under the banyan tree, surrounded by the village children, who listened to his tales as if they were magic spells. He looked up at the tree, its roots twisting deeply into the earth, its branches reaching wide into the sky. He felt a strange peace, a sense of completeness, as though he too were rooted into the heart of Thottakudi. "Do you see this tree?" he said to the children. "It has lived through more than any of us can imagine. And one day, you will sit here with your children and tell them stories. This tree will listen, just as it has listened to us. It will stand by you, sheltering your memories, binding you to this soil." The children looked up at the banyan tree, seeing it with new eyes, sensing the promise that had been handed down to them. In that moment, they understood that they were now part of the legacy of Thottakudi, the keepers of a heritage far older than themselves.

And as for the Collector, who had once viewed the banyan tree as an obstacle, he became one of its greatest champions. He often visited the village, bringing his own children to play under the tree. He'd sit with the villagers, sharing in the laughter, the stories, and the wisdom that floated under its branches. Over time, he grew to see the banyan tree not only as a piece of history, but as a lesson in humility—a reminder that progress is most meaningful when it honours what came before.

The banyan tree continued to stand, its leaves whispering secrets to the wind, its roots holding tight to the stories of

Thottakudi, a testament to the resilience of tradition and the strength of community. It grew not only as a tree but as a living memory, a place where generations met and found their place in the world, held together by the quiet, unwavering strength of the thatha maram, the Grandfather Tree.

Songs For Savithri

Savithri Amma's days in Hyderabad were quiet and routine, marked by the rustling of neem leaves and the distant bustle of the city. She had once been a singer of some repute, her voice a rich, mellifluous sound that filled temple halls and festival gatherings. Now, in her seventies, her voice lay dormant, a forgotten treasure nestled in the folds of memory. Her days were filled with hushed whispers of the past, conversations that existed only between herself and her small, south-facing room. Her son and daughter-in-law were busy with the relentless wheel of work and family life. Her grandchildren, though affectionate, had their eyes on mobile screens and voices tuned to their own worlds.

Each morning, Savithri Amma would sit by the open window, watching the skies pale and brighten as the city woke. She would gaze at the familiar sights—a lone crow perched on the neem branch, the milkman rattling his tin cans as he cycled through the lane, and the sudden surge of schoolchildren in their neatly pressed uniforms, chattering like sparrows as they hurried past. The warmth of the morning sun often brought a tune to her lips, a faint hum that arose almost unconsciously. It was during these quiet times, when her family was still in the midst of their morning routines, that she would let herself slip into fragments of old krithis and varnams, fragments of songs that now lay scattered like fragile petals on a windswept path.

One such morning, as Savithri Amma was humming "Mokshamu Galada," a soft but sharp tap on the window startled her. She turned and found herself face-to-face with a young man peering through the iron bars, a hopeful smile stretched across his face. "Excuse me,

Maaji," he said, his voice polite and respectful, with just a hint of excitement. "Is that...Tyagaraja that you're humming?"

Savithri Amma adjusted her saree pallu, startled but intrigued. "Yes, it is Tyagaraja. You recognize it?" Her tone carried the gentleness of curiosity mingled with disbelief, for in her household, her singing had become an artifact, a relic noticed only by the occasional passerby or housemaid.

The young man's face broke into a wider smile. "Yes, Maaji. I'm learning Carnatic music. Just moved here last week," he said, pointing towards the house next door. "My name is Akshay."

"Akshay," she repeated, tasting the syllables as if they were the notes of a raagam she was reacquainting herself with. "Carnatic music, you say?" Her eyes brightened as they hadn't in months, her mind conjuring images of the concert halls she had once graced, the ardent listeners she had once captivated.

"Yes, Maaji," he replied, sensing her interest. "I used to hear you humming every morning…at first, I thought I was imagining things. But your voice…" He hesitated, then continued, "It carries so much. It's not something one hears every day. You sing so well."

Savithri Amma chuckled, a gentle sound, like the swish of jasmine petals brushing against silk. "Once upon a time, yes," she admitted, with a modest wave of her hand, as though brushing aside her years of dedication and practice. "Now it's just…old habits." She glanced towards the hallway, instinctively listening for her family. "Akshay beta, you should focus on your studies. Why waste time listening to an old woman hum?"

But Akshay was undeterred. "Maaji, would you sing something for me? Just once? I would be honoured to hear you sing."

She hesitated, unused to such a request after so many silent years, yet something in his earnestness reminded her of her younger self, her own eagerness when she had learned under her first guru. She cast a glance down the hallway again, assured herself her son and daughter-in-law were occupied, and then, with a deep breath, began. She started with a soft alapana, her voice tentative at first, and then, as if awakening a sleeping giant, her voice bloomed, gaining strength and warmth as she navigated the intricate swaras with ease and grace. Akshay stood spellbound, his eyes wide with reverence and awe.

By the time she reached the charanam, her voice soared, filling the modest house with a richness it hadn't heard in years. As she finished, she realized her son, Karthik, stood at the end of the hallway, his eyes narrow with an unreadable expression.

"Amma, who are you singing for?" he asked, a slight edge to his voice.

Savithri Amma quickly drew her pallu over her shoulder, her moment of joy dimming. "This young man next door…he…he wanted to hear something. That's all." She managed a faint smile, but Karthik was already nodding, turning back to the kitchen.

"It's not a problem, Amma," he said. "But you should rest more. There's no need to tire yourself."

The words, though well-intended, left a faint sting. She had forgotten for a moment that her singing, once celebrated, was now considered just a curiosity, an indulgence of her old age. Akshay's voice broke her thoughts. "Maaji, please don't let my request be a bother. You sing beautifully. It's like…I don't know…I'm hearing the past come alive."

She waved her hand, dismissing his concern, but her heart was moved. "Thank you, beta. You are very kind," she said, a warmth returning to her eyes. "But, as my son said, it is time I took things easy."

But Akshay was persistent. Over the next few weeks, he would stop by in the mornings, catching her by the window, often with a request for a song or a question about some obscure raagam. Gradually, she found herself awaiting his visits, their impromptu lessons a small, unspoken ritual in her quiet life. She felt her voice returning, like a stream that had once dried up but now ran anew, nourished by the enthusiasm of a young, receptive mind.

One day, he brought her a small notebook, the edges frayed, its pages filled with lyrics he was learning. "Maaji, will you help me with these compositions?" he asked, his tone humble and hopeful.

She looked down at the notebook, her fingers grazing the worn cover. The touch brought a flood of memories— her own notebooks, filled with painstakingly noted swaras and annotations from her guru. "Akshay, you must learn to make each note your own," she advised, her voice soft but firm. "It is not about singing well but about feeling each line, each word."

In these shared moments, she felt the years fall away, her voice steady and strong, each note vibrating with the passion that had once been her lifeblood. She taught him with the patience of a mother, her heart swelling with pride as he improved, his youthful spirit breathing life into the words that had once meant the world to her.

One evening, as Akshay was preparing to leave, he looked at her with newfound respect. "Maaji, your family…do they know how lucky they are? You have so much to share, so much that even my teacher doesn't know."

Savithri Amma smiled, a sad yet accepting smile. "They are good people, Akshay. It's just… life is fast, you see. Everyone has their own tune, and sometimes, they forget the old ones." She gazed at the fading light, her thoughts a blend of contentment and melancholy.

What she didn't know was that her grandchildren, curious about the visitor next door, had begun to listen from the hallway, enchanted by the voice that had long been a lullaby in their lives but had gone unnoticed in the rush of routine. One evening, her granddaughter shyly approached her. "Patti, can you sing for me too?"

Savithri Amma's heart swelled, her voice catching as she nodded, the touch of her granddaughter's hand rekindling a long-buried hope. In that moment, she knew her voice would not remain silent much longer. And as she sang to the young girl, she felt the joy of shared song returning, a gift not only for herself but for all who had forgotten it could be a part of their lives.

As the days went on, Akshay's visits became the highlight of her routine, his presence a reminder of her past, a spark that reignited her joy for music. And slowly, like a song that takes root and spreads, her family began to notice, each in their own way, the small miracle taking place in their midst. Her daughter-in-law would pause by the door, listening to her sing; her son would stop reading the newspaper to catch a few bars of her morning practice. Even the neighbours started lingering by the gate, enchanted by the voice that had become the pulse of their quiet street.

In the gentle days that followed, Savithri Amma's house transformed. The silent walls and still rooms were no longer just a refuge for an aging woman; they had become the cradle of memories, melodies, and legacies—preserved in the simplest act of singing, shared now with those who mattered most.

Savithri Amma's song-filled mornings became a small beacon for the neighbourhood, an almost magical experience in an otherwise busy world. Akshay, her earnest young neighbour, continued to visit, often bringing her new pieces to sing or questions about the finer points of ragas. Their morning sessions became a ritual, and for Savithri Amma, these moments felt like a balm, a quiet rebellion against the silence her voice had been confined to over the years.

One breezy afternoon, her granddaughter Meera slipped into her room, shyly holding a notebook. She glanced around, as if to make sure they were alone, and then approached her grandmother with an endearing smile.

"Patti, I wrote something. Can you help me make it a song?"

Savithri Amma looked at her, heart swelling with pride and surprise. "A song, is it?" she asked, warmth filling her voice.

"Yes, Patti," Meera nodded, her eyes sparkling. "But I don't know how to sing it properly. Will you show me?"

The request was like a flicker of light in Savithri Amma's heart, rekindling her long-buried hope that her family, too, might find joy in the music that had once been her life's devotion. Taking the notebook from Meera, she read the young girl's simple, heartfelt words—about the changing seasons, the call of a cuckoo in the summer, the lull of the monsoon rains. Savithri Amma hummed the words softly, adjusting the rhythm to match the child's innocent verses, and soon, a lilting melody emerged, flowing like the gentle ripples of a calm river.

They spent the next hour crafting the song together, Meera listening wide-eyed as her grandmother explained how each note had a purpose, how each word could be shaped to evoke a feeling. When they were finished, Meera threw her arms around Savithri Amma's neck, whispering, "Thank you, Patti! I didn't know music was so…beautiful."

The joy of that moment lingered with Savithri Amma long after her granddaughter had skipped away, a quiet happiness settling over her like a familiar shawl on a cold evening. Yet, in the midst of this rekindled joy, Savithri Amma noticed a peculiar silence between herself and her son, Karthik. She could sense his restlessness, his glances that lingered longer than usual when he passed by her room, the way he occasionally sighed deeply as if burdened by something unspoken.

One evening, as she was tidying up after dinner, Karthik approached her in the kitchen. He seemed reluctant, unsure, as if struggling to find the right words.

"Amma, do you have a moment?" he finally asked, his tone unusually tentative.

She looked up, surprised by the seriousness in his voice. "Of course, kanna. What is it?"

Karthik hesitated, then spoke, choosing his words carefully. "I wanted to talk about… your singing. I know you're enjoying it, and it's nice to see you so happy." He paused, and she sensed there was a "but" looming.

"But?" she prodded gently, her eyes soft but keen.

He sighed, scratching the back of his neck, visibly uncomfortable. "I just… It's become a bit of a…distraction," he murmured, glancing down the hall as if to ensure they were alone. "The children are talking about it, and Meera…she's constantly asking to learn songs. And the neighbours… Amma, I don't mean to sound ungrateful, but I worry it's…drawing too much attention."

Savithri Amma listened, a pang of hurt blooming in her chest, though she kept her expression serene. "Distraction?" she echoed quietly, her tone questioning but not accusatory. "My singing is a distraction?"

Karthik shifted his weight uncomfortably. "You know what I mean, Amma. We've moved on from those days.

There's so much to manage, and with you singing more, it feels like the children are focusing less on studies, and more on…" He trailed off, sensing he'd already said too much.

Savithri Amma lowered her gaze, nodding slowly, her fingers gently twisting the end of her saree. The quiet joy that had blossomed in her life, shared with her grandchildren and her new friend Akshay, suddenly felt fragile, as if it could crumble under the weight of her son's words. She forced a gentle smile. "I understand, Karthik. Don't worry. I'll be more careful."

Karthik looked relieved, even grateful, patting her shoulder gently before heading off. But as he left, Savithri Amma felt a subtle chill in the air, a reminder that the world she now lived in no longer cherished music as it once had.

For the next few days, she fell silent. When Akshay came by, she would offer him a polite smile and a nod but little else. He noticed her withdrawn demeanour, the way she avoided eye contact and only spoke when necessary. Eventually, he decided to ask.

"Maaji, did I do something to offend you?" he asked, standing at the window one morning with a cautious look in his eyes.

Savithri Amma shook her head, her gaze distant. "No, Akshay beta. You've done nothing wrong. It's just…sometimes, it is best not to disturb others. Singing has become a thing of the past, a relic. My family, they have other matters to focus on. I don't want to cause trouble."

Akshay's face softened with understanding, and a slight hint of defiance. "But, Maaji, music isn't just sound. It's life…you bring something to this place that no one else can. It's not disturbing anyone. If anything, it's…" He paused, searching for the right word. "It's reminding us all of something precious."

She listened, the quiet fire of his words stirring something within her. But her heart remained weighed down by her son's words. She nodded politely, not wanting to prolong the conversation. Seeing her determination to withdraw, Akshay sighed, his shoulders slumping in disappointment.

It was Meera, her granddaughter, who reignited her spirit with a simple act. One evening, Savithri Amma found Meera practicing the song they'd created together, her voice soft but filled with a raw sweetness. The young girl faltered, missing a note, but continued singing with unwavering resolve. The sound was tender, each note a tribute to the connection they had shared.

Moved, Savithri Amma sat down beside her. "Singing isn't easy, is it, kanna?" she murmured, her voice barely a whisper.

Meera looked up, her eyes wide with innocent determination. "It's hard, but you taught me, Patti. If I don't try, how will I learn?"

Tears pricked Savithri Amma's eyes. She pulled Meera close, her heart swelling with a fierce pride. "You're right, my dear," she said softly. "Never stop trying, even if it feels hard. And always, always follow what brings you joy."

The next day, Savithri Amma stood by the window, gazing at the familiar street, her mind swirling with thoughts. She realized that her love for music, for singing, was not just a personal pleasure—it was a legacy, one that she was meant to pass on, whether her son approved or not. She knew, too, that while her family's concerns came from a place of love, they couldn't understand what music meant to her, nor the joy it brought to those who heard it.

With newfound resolve, she decided to resume her morning sessions with Akshay, not just for his sake but for her own. She wanted to remind herself, her family, and her neighbours that the soul of a person is never truly silent, even if others fail to hear its melody. She would be respectful of her family's wishes, careful not to overstep, but she would not let her voice fade into silence again.

The following morning, as the sun's first rays kissed the neem leaves outside her window, she began a soft alapana, her voice rising like the morning light itself. Her heart swelled with emotion as she sang, each note a proclamation that she was still here, still capable of beauty, still worthy of being heard. As she sang, she noticed Meera peeking around the corner, her face beaming with pride, while Akshay stood outside, listening with his usual reverence.

In that moment, Savithri Amma knew that even if her son didn't understand, even if the world around her was too busy to pause and listen, she would continue to sing— not just for herself, but for those who had begun to hear the song she carried within her. For in her heart, she knew that her voice was not just hers; it was a gift she would leave behind, a gift her family and her community would one day come to cherish.

And thus, as her voice filled the morning air, she found herself filled with a renewed purpose—a purpose that she would carry forward, a song of resilience and grace that would echo long after she was gone.

Over the weeks that followed, Savithri Amma's voice returned to the neighbourhood with a gentle but unmistakable strength. She resumed her sessions with Akshay, guiding him through the intricate nuances of the ragas, her once-timid notes growing fuller and more assured with each passing day. The neighbours, too, had begun to notice and, curiously, no longer seemed bothered by her singing. Instead, her morning practice became a part of the neighbourhood's routine—a familiar backdrop that evoked a shared nostalgia among the residents.

Yet in the midst of this newfound appreciation, her son Karthik's unease lingered. He noticed the neighbours lingering outside their windows or pausing as they passed by, listening with quiet admiration. Though their reactions were mostly positive, he still felt uneasy, caught between his mother's happiness and his own concerns about what people might think.

One evening, after dinner, Karthik gathered the family in the living room. He wanted to speak with his mother openly, though he wasn't quite sure how to voice his concerns without wounding her. Savithri Amma sensed his discomfort and waited patiently, her gentle smile encouraging him to continue.

"Amma," he began slowly, choosing his words carefully, "I see how much singing means to you, and I understand that it brings you happiness. But…" He paused, glancing toward his wife, who nodded subtly. "I worry that it's affecting the children's focus and maybe even how others view our family. People may see it as… unusual."

Savithri Amma took a deep breath, steadying herself. She looked at her son, her eyes filled with a quiet determination. "Karthik, I understand that you worry about what people think. But I'm not doing this to gain attention or disturb anyone. Singing is a part of who I am—just as much as this family is. If my singing can bring even a small amount of joy, isn't that worth something?"

Karthik looked away, unable to meet her gaze. "But Amma, times have changed. People don't understand the way they used to. They might think…"

"That I'm strange? That I should be silent?" Savithri Amma's voice was firm but tender. She took his hand gently. "Kanna, I know you have your reasons for wanting things to be a certain way. But let me remind you that sometimes, traditions and talents shouldn't fade just because the world moves faster. They remind us of who we are."

Just then, Meera, who had been listening quietly in the corner, spoke up. "Appa, I love it when Patti sings. It makes our house feel warm and happy. And when she teaches me songs, it feels like…she's sharing something precious with me."

Karthik looked at his daughter, his expression softening. "You feel that way, Meera?"

"Yes, Appa. And my friends at school think it's amazing that Patti sings so beautifully. They ask me to sing the songs she taught me."

The family fell silent, Karthik contemplating his daughter's words. Perhaps, he realized, he had underestimated the value his mother's singing brought, not just to the household but to the children as well. He looked at Savithri Amma, his eyes conveying a quiet acceptance, as if he was beginning to see her in a new light.

The turning point came during the festival of Navaratri. As per tradition, the women in their neighbourhood visited each other's homes to view the "golu" displays—ornate arrangements of dolls that symbolized divine figures, cultural icons, and beloved legends. This year, however, their neighbourhood association had planned something special—a small music program to celebrate the festival.

One morning, as Savithri Amma was busy arranging her dolls, the head of the association, Mrs. Nirmala, came by with a warm smile. "Savithri Amma," she began, folding her hands respectfully, "we've heard so much about your beautiful voice. Would you honour us by singing a few songs for the Navaratri program?"

Savithri Amma felt a surge of both joy and apprehension. It had been years since she'd sung before an audience. While she had regained confidence through her sessions with Akshay, the thought of performing in front of others was daunting.

"Oh, I don't know…" she replied, hesitating. "I'm not sure I'm ready to sing before a crowd."

Akshay, who had come by to practice that morning, overheard the conversation and immediately stepped in. "Of course she'll sing, aunty! She sings every morning, and the whole neighbourhood loves it. This is a chance for everyone to enjoy her music."

Savithri Amma looked at Akshay, his enthusiasm bolstering her courage. Slowly, she nodded. "Alright, I'll sing. But only if you'll accompany me on the tanpura."

Akshay beamed, nodding eagerly. "I'd be honoured, Maaji."

Word quickly spread, and by the evening of the program, the small community hall was filled with neighbours, young and old, who had come to listen. Karthik and his family sat in the front row, Meera clutching her father's hand excitedly. Even Karthik, though still slightly hesitant, watched his mother with newfound pride.

Savithri Amma took her place on the stage, her heart beating fast as she glanced at the expectant faces before her. She closed her eyes, took a deep breath, and began with a soulful alapana, her voice unfurling like a delicate flower, filling the hall with warmth and serenity. Akshay played the tanpura steadily beside her, his young hands steady and reverent as he supported her with each note.

As she moved into the main raga, the hall seemed to melt away, and she was transported back to her younger years, to memories of her guru's guidance, of her first performance, of the boundless joy that singing had always brought her. Her voice rose and fell, each note resonating deeply, evoking emotions that lay dormant within the listeners.

When she finished, there was a moment of complete, awed silence before the hall erupted in applause. Tears of joy filled her eyes as she looked out at the audience, her family's faces radiant with pride. Meera rushed up to the stage, throwing her arms around her grandmother, while Karthik, moved beyond words, stood clapping with all his heart.

Later that night, as the family walked home together, Karthik gently took his mother's hand. "Amma, I'm sorry for doubting you. I never realized how much this means—not just to you, but to all of us. You've given us something beautiful, something that can't be replaced."

Savithri Amma looked at him, her heart filled with love. "Karthik, music is a gift that should be shared. Just as you teach your children values, I wanted to share what I know with you and them. I don't sing to make you uncomfortable—I sing to keep the family's spirit alive."

Karthik nodded, understanding at last. "Thank you, Amma. Thank you for reminding us of what really matters."

In the days that followed, her morning practice continued, but now, it was no longer just a solitary exercise. Often, Meera would join her, sitting by her side and learning the intricate art of each raga. Her family, too, would linger nearby, appreciating the beauty of her songs, their hearts warmed by the sound of her voice. Neighbours paused to listen, and even passersby would stop to catch a few notes, touched by the grace and strength of her music.

Savithri Amma's song became the soul of the neighbourhood, a reminder of heritage, of resilience, and of the power that even a single voice could hold in the lives of many. And so, as the seasons turned and her voice continued to weave its way through each dawn, the once-silent home became alive with melody, laughter, and a legacy that would endure long after she was gone.

The Forgotten Dance

Gowri sat in the cool shade of her verandah in Madurai, a faint smile playing at her lips as she watched the world go by. It was mid-morning, and sunlight filtered gently through the neem trees, dappling the dusty lane with flecks of gold. Vendors called out their wares, bicycles clattered over cobblestones, and now and then, a flock of sparrows would sweep by, chirping in cheerful abandon.

The house had been Gowri's home for over forty years, a silent witness to her life's story. She remembered the vibrant celebrations and gatherings, the walls echoing with laughter. Now, in her retirement, the house was quieter. Her daughter had moved abroad, her son, though diligent in calling her every weekend, was in Chennai. Gowri filled her days with cooking, sewing, and tending to the small vegetable patch behind the house. She had settled comfortably into this solitude, or so she thought.

This particular morning, however, was different. Her old friends from her youth—Radhika, Leela, and Sumathi—were visiting. Their husbands had retired as well, and they, too, were grandmothers with daughters and sons scattered far and wide. The old friends had taken to visiting one another once in a while, each visit a chance to relive the long-forgotten days of their youth.

"Gowri, do you remember our last Bharatanatyam performance in college?" Radhika asked, laughter twinkling in her eyes. "How could she forget?" Leela chimed in, "She was the star! The way she moved... the whole audience was spellbound!"

Gowri shifted uneasily, a slight flush colouring her cheeks. The memory stirred inside her like an old tune. She had been known for her graceful Bharatanatyam performances, her elegance evident in every mudra and step. But all of that was a lifetime ago. When she married Sundaram, a schoolteacher from a respected family, her dancing days ended. She gave her dreams a quiet farewell, dedicating herself to her family, as was expected. In truth, she had grown accustomed to her life without dance, but her friends' words stirred a pang of yearning she had long suppressed.

Sumathi leaned forward, her eyes alight with mischief. "What if you danced again? Just once. For old times' sake?"

"Oh, don't be absurd!" Gowri said, brushing off the suggestion with a small laugh. "Who would want to see an old lady like me stumbling around?"

But her friends were insistent, their cajoling relentless. "The children of this generation have never seen a proper Bharatanatyam performance!" Radhika said. "They don't know what they're missing!"

"Yes, think of it, Gowri! You'd be introducing them to something beautiful, something that connects them to their roots," added Leela, nodding eagerly.

Gowri sighed, hoping to divert the conversation. But the idea had already taken root, and her friends wouldn't let it be. They concocted a plan: Gowri would perform for the neighbourhood children. Word would be spread discreetly among the residents, and a small crowd would gather in the little courtyard outside her house. It would be an intimate affair, they promised, nothing elaborate.

The idea settled in Gowri's mind as she went about her day. That night, she found herself glancing at an old, worn-out photograph on her shelf, tucked among pictures of her children and grandchildren. In it, she was dressed in a Bharatanatyam costume, young and radiant, her eyes alive with dreams and possibilities. She traced the outline of the photo with a wistful finger.

The next morning, as she dusted her shelves, a realization swept over her: she could barely remember the steps. Years of discipline, rigor, and passion were now locked away, gathering dust like her memories. The thought saddened her, but there was also a flicker of defiance. What harm was there in trying?

With that resolve, Gowri decided to practice, if only for her own satisfaction. She went into her small room and carefully locked the door. Taking a deep breath, she stood in the centre, her hands gracefully poised, her feet positioned as they had been countless times before. She closed her eyes, trying to recall the beat, the rhythm that had once been second nature to her. Slowly, hesitantly, she began to move.

At first, her steps were awkward, her movements jerky. Her body resisted, unfamiliar with these forgotten patterns. But as she persisted, something within her began to awaken. Her limbs loosened, her steps grew more fluid, and a soft smile appeared on her face. She was no longer the retired schoolteacher, shuffling through her garden; she was Gowri, the dancer, the young woman with stars in her eyes.

In the days that followed, her friends would visit, bringing gossip and laughter, but never mentioning the performance. It became an unspoken secret between them. Gowri would continue her quiet rehearsals in the solitude of her room, and with each practice, she found herself shedding years of restraint, tapping into a deep well of joy she had almost forgotten existed.

On the evening of the performance, Radhika, Leela, and Sumathi arrived early, armed with trays of sweets and savoury snacks. They bustled about, arranging chairs in the courtyard and decorating the small stage they had set up with strings of jasmine and marigold. Word had spread among the neighbourhood children, who came with curious faces and eager whispers.

When Gowri finally emerged, dressed in a simple yet elegant saree, her hands trembling slightly, a murmur of admiration swept through the crowd. The children, unused to seeing the soft-spoken old lady in such a poised manner, stared at her with wide eyes.

Radhika gave her a reassuring nod, and Gowri took her place at the centre of the makeshift stage. She took a deep breath, raising her hands gracefully, and began. The familiar rhythm filled the air, her movements slow and measured at first, gaining confidence as she went on. Her friends clapped softly in time, and even the children, unused to this kind of performance, began to watch in awe.

Gowri danced as if she were a young girl again, her heart brimming with unspoken stories. Each gesture, each expression held the weight of years, the triumphs and sorrows she had endured in silence. For a brief moment, she was not just Gowri—the mother, the grandmother, the retired teacher. She was Gowri, the dancer, with all her passions and dreams laid bare for the world to see.

As she completed the final step, the courtyard erupted in applause. Gowri looked around, slightly dazed, her heart still racing from the dance. The children stared up at her with something like reverence, and her friends were smiling with a deep satisfaction. Gowri felt tears pricking her eyes, overwhelmed by the sudden rush of emotions.

One young girl stepped forward, her eyes wide with admiration. "Aunty, will you teach me to dance?"

Gowri laughed softly, bending down to touch the girl's cheek. "Perhaps," she replied, her voice gentle but full of promise. In that moment, she felt as though she had found something precious, something she hadn't even known she had lost.

This performance was more than a dance; it was a rekindling of her spirit. Gowri could see that the children were spellbound, their young faces transformed with newfound respect. For the first time, they saw her not as a quiet, ordinary woman, but as a bearer of a tradition that bridged past and present.

The days following the performance were unlike anything Gowri had experienced in years. Word spread throughout the neighbourhood about the "dancing teacher," as the children affectionately called her now. Everywhere she went—the vegetable market, the temple, even in her quiet strolls down the street—she received admiring glances and polite nods. The young girl who had approached her after the performance, Lalitha, had come to her doorstep the very next morning, asking to learn Bharatanatyam.

"Please, Aunty!" she had pleaded, her hands pressed together in a perfect namaskaram, eyes shining with anticipation. "Teach me, even if just a little."

It had been a long time since Gowri had considered herself a teacher of anything other than Tamil grammar and arithmetic. Yet, in Lalitha's earnest request, she sensed a flicker of something familiar—a passion, a hunger that mirrored her own youthful love for dance. Though hesitant at first, Gowri found herself agreeing, her heart-warming with an inexplicable joy.

Thus, every evening as the sun dipped below the rooftops of Madurai, Lalitha would arrive at Gowri's doorstep, her feet bare and eager, eyes full of excitement. Other children soon joined her, shyly at first, curious about the "aunty who danced." Before long, Gowri had a small gathering of students—a mix of girls and boys, all eager to learn the intricate art of Bharatanatyam.

As the children gathered around, Gowri would begin each lesson with the simplest of steps, explaining the meaning of every movement, every mudra. Her voice was steady and calm as she recounted stories of gods and goddesses, tales of valour, devotion, and sacrifice. Bharatanatyam, she told them, was more than just dance; it was a form of storytelling, a way to convey the innermost emotions through the language of movement.

Days turned into weeks, and Gowri found herself looking forward to each class. The children's laughter filled her courtyard, their feet tapping in unison on the earth, their faces earnest as they attempted to mirror her every move. Gowri's friends often watched from the sidelines, smiling at her newfound energy, their laughter mingling with the children's giggles.

One evening, as she guided Lalitha through a particularly graceful pose, Gowri noticed a figure watching from a distance. She squinted and recognized him—Murugan, the neighbourhood's handyman, who did odd jobs around the temple and often helped with repairs in the area. He was a man of few words, respected for his honesty and hardworking nature, but not known for lingering or watching anything that didn't concern him.

Seeing him standing there, his eyes fixed on her class, Gowri hesitated. She thought perhaps he had come to ask about some repair, so she excused herself from the children and approached him.

"Murugan, is there something you need?" she asked gently.

Murugan shifted awkwardly, scratching the back of his head. "Madam… I… I was just watching the children. It reminded me of… when I was young."

Gowri raised her eyebrows, intrigued. "Did you also dance, Murugan?"

Murugan laughed, a low, embarrassed sound. "Not dance, madam. But my mother, she used to sing. She taught me to keep rhythm with the tabla. I stopped after she passed away." He fell silent, staring at the ground as if embarrassed by his confession.

A thought crossed Gowri's mind. "Would you like to join us, Murugan?" she asked, surprising herself.

Murugan looked up, his eyes wide with disbelief. "Me? I... I couldn't... what would the children think?"

But Gowri only smiled, waving away his concerns. "The children would love it, and so would I. Bharatanatyam is not only about dance; rhythm and music are just as important."

From that day on, Murugan became a quiet yet steadfast part of their little gathering. While the children practiced their steps, he would sit on a small stool at the edge of the courtyard, keeping time with an old wooden tabla he had dusted off and brought along. His beats were steady, grounding the children's movements, adding a new depth to their learning.

One evening, as Gowri watched the children dance to the rhythm of Murugan's tabla, a memory surfaced in her mind—a memory of her own youth, when she had performed on grand stages, accompanied by a full orchestra. She recalled the rush of excitement, the thrill of stepping onto the stage, feeling the eyes of an audience fixed upon her. She realized, with a pang, how much she had missed that feeling, that sense of being seen, of being truly understood.

The children, meanwhile, began to adore Murugan. To them, he was an exotic figure, a gentle giant with hands that could coax melodies from the simplest of beats. Gowri watched as the children's eyes widened with awe when Murugan showed them how to mimic the beat by tapping their feet or clapping their hands. He shared stories of his own mother, of the old festivals where he had once played in local gatherings. Gowri saw that he, too, was finding something in these classes—a way to reconnect with his own past, a chance to revive the forgotten traditions he had once cherished.

One evening, after the children had left, Murugan stayed behind, helping Gowri tidy up the courtyard. As they worked in companionable silence, he suddenly looked up and said, "Madam, thank you. You've given me something I didn't know I needed."

Gowri smiled, feeling a sense of gratitude herself. "You remind me of my younger days too, Murugan. Teaching you all... it has brought me a happiness I had long forgotten."

As the months passed, the dance classes became a cherished ritual for the entire neighbourhood. Even the adults would gather at a distance, their faces lit up with fond amusement, watching their children immerse themselves in a world that, in many ways, felt like a bridge to the past.

One day, during a particularly animated practice, Lalitha tugged at Gowri's saree. "Aunty, will you dance for us again? Like you did that first day?"

The other children chimed in, their voices eager, pleading. Murugan, too, looked at her, his face breaking into an encouraging smile.

Gowri hesitated, feeling the old pang of self-doubt. She was no longer the young dancer who could command a stage; age had tempered her movements, and her steps were not as agile as they once were. But seeing the children's hopeful faces, she felt a gentle urging within her, a quiet voice telling her that perhaps this was what she was meant to do—to share her joy of dance, regardless of age or skill.

She nodded, a soft smile spreading across her face, and stepped forward. The children sat in a circle around her, their eyes wide with anticipation. Murugan began the rhythm on his tabla, slow and measured, and Gowri closed her eyes, letting herself sink into the familiar cadence. She began with a simple pose, her hands and feet moving gracefully, each movement imbued with a lifetime of memories.

As she danced, she felt a surge of energy, a warmth spreading through her veins. She could see, out of the corner of her eye, the children watching her with rapt attention, their expressions a mixture of awe and reverence. She felt as if she were offering them a gift—a glimpse into a world they had never known, a world where dance and tradition were interwoven with every fibre of her being.

When she finally stopped, breathless and flushed, the children burst into applause, their small hands clapping with unbridled joy. Gowri looked around, her heart swelling with pride and gratitude. For the first time in many years, she felt whole, her soul alive with the music of her youth.

In the quiet that followed, Lalitha spoke up, her voice soft but firm. "Aunty, can we have a real performance? One where the whole neighbourhood can come and watch?"

The other children nodded enthusiastically, their eyes shining with excitement.

Gowri looked around, a spark of mischief glinting in her eyes. "Well, if you're all willing to practice hard, perhaps we can put on a proper show," she said, her voice light with laughter.

And so, a plan was set in motion—a grand performance, one that would bring together the young and the old, binding them with the shared joy of tradition, rhythm, and dance.

The weeks leading up to the performance were a blur of activity. Every evening, the courtyard rang with laughter and the slap of bare feet on stone as the children practiced with boundless enthusiasm. Murugan's rhythmic drumming filled the air, and Gowri's voice rose over it all, giving instructions, adjusting poses, and recounting stories from myth and legend to bring each gesture to life.

The whole neighbourhood seemed to be caught up in the excitement. Word had spread beyond Gowri's street, and parents from other lanes came by to watch, their curiosity piqued. Some of the elders even joined the practice sessions, bringing small snacks for the children and sharing stories of their own youthful days. Gowri felt an inexplicable joy, a sense of fulfilment that warmed her heart each night as she watched the children absorb themselves in Bharatanatyam.

Soon, the day of the performance arrived. The entire neighbourhood gathered in the courtyard, transformed for the occasion with strings of jasmine, marigold garlands, and a modest platform for a stage. Lamps were lit, casting a soft, golden glow over the gathering, and a gentle evening breeze rustled through the leaves, carrying the scent of incense and fresh flowers.

Gowri stood behind the makeshift curtain, her heart thudding with a mixture of excitement and nerves. She peeked out at the audience, scanning the sea of familiar faces and marvelling at the sight. There were neighbours, friends, and even passersby who had been drawn to the event. She spotted Radhika, Leela, and Sumathi in the front row, their faces bright with pride and encouragement.

As the children took their places on stage, Gowri gave them a reassuring nod. They were dressed in simple, colourful costumes that she and her friends had sewn together over the past few weeks. Lalitha stood at the front, her eyes sparkling with anticipation. Murugan, sitting by the stage, adjusted his tabla, his fingers poised to begin.

When the music started, a hush fell over the crowd. The children moved with a surprising grace, their young faces intense and focused, as they executed each step and gesture Gowri had painstakingly taught them. Gowri watched them, her heart swelling with pride. The children's dance was simple, yet it carried with it a charm and sincerity that moved the audience deeply. She could see the faces in the crowd, transfixed by the rhythm, captivated by the sight of these young dancers bringing an ancient art to life.

Then came the final act, one that the children had insisted on, much to Gowri's initial reluctance. She was to join them on stage, to dance alongside them for the finale. It was an idea she had resisted fiercely, fearing that she would not be able to keep pace with the youthful energy of her students. But their persistence—and her own growing joy in rediscovering dance—had softened her resolve. As she stepped onto the stage, a soft murmur ran through the crowd. Dressed in a simple, elegant saree, her hair adorned with a single jasmine strand, Gowri looked out at the audience, her heart pounding. She raised her hands, signalling the start of her dance, and Murugan struck the first beat on the tabla.

Gowri moved with the ease of one who had danced these steps in her very bones. Though slower, her movements were imbued with a lifetime of emotion and wisdom. Every turn of her wrist, every tilt of her head conveyed not just the story of the dance but the journey of her own life—the sacrifices, the love, the passion that she had set aside, and the joy she had now reclaimed.

As she danced, a hush fell over the audience, the only sound the soft beat of the tabla and the gentle swish of her saree. The children watched her with rapt attention, their eyes wide with admiration, mirroring the awe of the crowd. In that moment, Gowri felt a profound connection—a bridge between her world and theirs, between the traditions of the past and the possibilities of the future.

The performance ended with Gowri holding the final pose, her hands gracefully poised in front of her, her face serene yet glowing. For a moment, there was silence, as if the entire gathering was holding its breath. Then, slowly, the applause began, growing in waves until the whole courtyard resounded with claps and cheers.

Gowri looked around, overwhelmed by the response, a deep sense of fulfilment warming her heart. Lalitha ran up to her and wrapped her arms around her waist, her small face beaming with pride. Murugan nodded at her, his smile wide and genuine, his eyes bright with admiration. Her friends were cheering from the front row, their hands clapping wildly, faces lit with pride and joy.

As the crowd slowly dispersed, people came up to Gowri, expressing their admiration, their gratitude. Some of the parents shared stories of their own childhoods, of grandparents and parents who had once danced, sung, or performed. It was as if Gowri's dance had rekindled memories in each of them, weaving together their shared heritage and reminding them of the beauty of their traditions. Late that night, after everyone had left and the lamps had been extinguished, Gowri sat in her courtyard, her heart still full. She looked up at the stars, feeling as if her spirit had been lifted, her life expanded in ways she had never thought possible. She realized that, in rekindling her love for dance, she had not only revived a forgotten part of herself but had given the children— and indeed the whole neighbourhood—a glimpse into the richness of their heritage.

The next morning, Lalitha and a few of the other children appeared at her doorstep, their faces expectant. "Aunty," Lalitha said, "can we practice again today?" Gowri laughed, her heart swelling with a joy she hadn't felt in years. She gathered them into the courtyard, knowing that she had found her calling once more. Bharatanatyam had not only returned to her life but had also become a bridge that connected generations, a legacy she could pass on. In the days that followed, her courtyard was never empty. The laughter of children, the soft rhythm of the tabla, and the gentle thud of footsteps became a part of her daily life, a symphony of sounds that filled her with gratitude.

And so, in that small courtyard in Madurai, under the watchful eyes of friends and neighbours, Gowri danced on—no longer alone, but surrounded by the future, by children who would carry forward the beauty of an art that was, after all, timeless.

Letters From The Past

The sunlight slanted through the window of Krishna's modest home, casting a golden glow over the stack of books and papers that lay scattered across the floor. Krishna's old, creaking wooden almirah was open, its contents half-emptied in a chaotic pile. He had set out to find his passport for his son, but as the hours stretched, he had found instead a world of lost memories, buried beneath layers of documents, yellowing photographs, and letters.

And then, there it was—a box bound in worn brown string, tucked far behind the other papers. Krishna pulled it out with a puzzled frown, tracing his wrinkled fingers along the cardboard edges. The box smelled faintly of old paper and a time long passed. He untied the string carefully, as if unwrapping a long-lost treasure, and lifted the lid. Inside, letters were stacked—faded, folded, some with delicate edges curling with age. His fingers trembled as he lifted the first one. He hadn't realized he'd kept these.

He looked down at the familiar handwriting on the envelope—his own, from many years ago, written with the careful, slanting strokes of a young man in love. To my beloved Radhika. His heart thudded, both at the weight of nostalgia and at the tender, gentle ache that the mere thought of her name still invoked. Radhika had been gone for three years now, yet the essence of her— the laughter that had filled their days, the warmth she'd brought to their small home—lingered still, as vibrant as if she were right beside him.

Krishna settled himself down on the floor, not minding the ache in his knees, and unfolded the letter.

"Radhika," he read softly, as if speaking to her across the years, "there is no one like you in this whole world. Every time I think of you, I feel as if I'm back at Marina Beach, sitting under the stars, watching the waves. You make me feel like the ocean—you make me feel endless."

The words seemed foreign, almost grandiose, coming from his mouth. But as he read on, Krishna remembered. He had been a clerk in the Chennai office of the Railways then, a young man with big dreams and a heart full of love for a girl with flowers in her hair and laughter like the monsoon rain. How much he had wanted to give her the world, though all he had managed was a modest life in a small flat in T. Nagar. Radhika had never complained. She had only smiled and worked beside him to make that life their own.

He read on, letter after letter, each one peeling back layers of his past, filled with both joy and the ordinary troubles of married life. They wrote to each other about the smallest things—the price of rice, her mother's health, the arrival of their first child, Ravi. He remembered how Radhika would sprinkle jasmine in her hair and hum softly as she cooked, or how she would sit at the edge of the bed, waiting for him with a steaming cup of coffee.

The sun had shifted by the time Krishna's daughter, Anita, came into the room. Her face softened as she saw him, her father's gaze lost in those brittle letters. It had been difficult for him, Anita knew, since her mother's passing. Her father was a proud man, and grief was something he wore in silence. They all missed her, but for Krishna, Radhika had been the whole rhythm of his life, the gentle balance that held him steady.

"Appa?" she asked gently, touching his shoulder. Krishna looked up, blinking as if waking from a dream.

"These letters," he murmured, holding them up for her to see. "I wrote these to your mother. I didn't even remember keeping them."

Anita sat down beside him, curiosity flickering in her eyes as she took one of the letters, her mother's name written in her father's youthful handwriting. As she read the words aloud, a soft smile broke across her face. The letter spoke of long days at work, of the food Radhika packed for him, of his hopes for their future, and his joy at coming home to her each evening.

"He never told us about any of this," she said, glancing at her father. "You were always so quiet, Appa. Who knew you had this kind of romance in you?"

Krishna laughed, a deep, almost embarrassed chuckle. "It was different back then. I may not have had grand words, but your mother knew. She always knew."

Anita read through a few more letters, each one like a window into her parents' lives. As a child, she had never thought much about the love that connected them, but seeing it in black and white, woven through the years, she began to realize how much her father had loved her mother, not just with words but with a steady devotion that was woven into the fabric of their family.

Days passed, and Krishna found himself absorbed in these letters. Every afternoon, he would take one or two out to read, each one like rediscovering his youth. He thought of their early years—the late nights, the quarrels, the laughter that always returned, binding them closer. Each letter held a piece of their story, and with each one,

Krishna's heart filled with memories of a life he had almost forgotten.

One evening, Anita brought her brother, Ravi, over to listen as Krishna read one of the letters aloud. Ravi leaned back against the wall, listening intently as his father's words unfurled the tale of his own youth. He found himself marvelling at this softer, more vulnerable side of the father he'd always thought so stoic.

"Appa," Ravi said after a moment of silence. "You never really told us what it was like, being young and in love with Amma."

Krishna smiled, looking into the distance, his thoughts drifting back. "Your mother was... what can I say? She was everything. I was just a simple man with a stable job and a few dreams, but Radhika—she made everything brighter. She was like sunlight, filling the house with her warmth. She would wait by the door each evening, a smile on her face as if that was all she had waited for, all day long."

Anita felt a lump rise in her throat, picturing her mother's smiling face, that familiar warmth that had lit up their home. Her parents had lived through so much together—the tight months when Krishna's income was all they had, the sicknesses, the milestones. And yet, they had kept going, their bond strengthening as the years wore on.

"Do you remember that time we all went to Mylapore?" Krishna asked them, his eyes twinkling. "Your mother had this sudden idea to visit the temple, and she dragged us all along, even though I had told her we couldn't afford the extra expense. She bought sweets and small trinkets, insisting on treating each of you. She always had a way of making moments feel special."

Ravi laughed, nodding. "And we got caught in the rain on the way back! Amma pulled us under a tree, but it barely kept us dry."

"Yes, and your mother laughed the whole time," Krishna chuckled. "I remember her standing there, soaked and smiling. She always found joy in small things, even when I couldn't see it."

The memory hung in the room, thick with emotion, the years rolling back to that rainy afternoon. Through these letters and memories, Krishna's children began to see their parents not just as Amma and Appa but as Radhika and Krishna, two young people who had fallen in love and built a life together.

Krishna's voice grew softer as he continued reading. "Radhika," he read, "whatever happens in this life, know that you are my greatest blessing. You make my small world feel big. With you, I feel as if I have everything."

Anita and Ravi sat there in silence, struck by the depth of their father's words. They felt a newfound respect for the quiet, enduring love that had bound their parents together. They had seen their parents grow old, but now, they were seeing them anew—as young lovers, as people who had laughed and struggled, as individuals who had chosen to build a life together with both joy and sacrifice.

Later that night, as Krishna put the letters back in the box, he felt a sense of peace he hadn't known in years. In these letters, he had found more than memories; he had found his Radhika again, not just in the faded ink but in the love that filled their home, now carried on by their children.

As he tied the box shut and placed it carefully on the shelf, Krishna felt as though a part of him had come full circle. The letters were his past, but they were also his present—a reminder of the love that had built their family and continued to live on, quietly and beautifully, in every corner of his life.

Krishna sat at his desk the following evening, the bundle of letters spread before him. The events of the previous day felt like a kind of awakening, as if he'd not only rediscovered Radhika but also, in a way, himself. He thought he'd forgotten those days when he and Radhika were young, but it seemed they had only lain dormant, buried beneath the day-to-day routines of family life.

As he fingered the delicate edges of a yellowed envelope, he recalled the story of this particular letter. It was written during a time when he and Radhika had just moved into their first flat in Chennai. They'd been married only a few months, and everything felt new, from the sounds of the bustling street outside to the way their voices echoed in the empty, unfurnished rooms. Life was unsteady then—his railway job just barely met their needs, and Krishna remembered the worry that sometimes clouded Radhika's gaze, though she had always tried to hide it.

He opened the letter and began to read.

"Radhika," he read aloud, "I know I don't have much to offer. All I can give you is my promise that I'll always try my best to keep you happy. Every time I see your smile, I feel as though I've accomplished something worthwhile.

I know you wanted a bigger place, a nicer view, but give me time. Someday, I'll make it happen for us."

Krishna chuckled, shaking his head. How young he had been then, how full of ambition. And how patient Radhika had been, always waving away his concerns with a light laugh, as if to say, "What does it matter? As long as we're together."

His mind wandered back to that first flat—the thin walls, the cracked tiles in the kitchen, and Radhika laughing at the drip-drip of a leaky tap that had driven him to exasperation. She would throw open the windows, letting the city sounds spill in, as if the world were singing just for them. Her love had always been simple, unburdened by expectations.

Krishna's reverie was broken by a soft knock. It was his granddaughter, Priya, peering into the room with wide, curious eyes. At nine years old, she was already sharp-witted, always observing the adults around her with a knowing, almost mischievous smile.

"Thatha, what are you reading?" she asked, tilting her head with interest.

Krishna smiled, gesturing for her to sit beside him. "I'm reading some old letters I wrote to your Paati," he explained. "These were from many years ago, before you were even born."

Priya's eyes widened with wonder. "You wrote letters to Paati?"

"Yes," he replied with a chuckle. "Back then, there were no phones or messages like you have today. Letters were the only way we shared our thoughts. Each one took time and care."

She looked at him in awe, as if letters were relics from a distant age of kings and queens. "Will you read me one, Thatha?" she asked eagerly.

Krishna hesitated, then nodded. He chose a lighter letter, one filled with the small joys and teases he used to share with Radhika. Clearing his throat, he began to read:

"Dear Radhika, yesterday I bought you a jasmine garland on my way home, but by the time I arrived, the flowers had all wilted. You told me it was fine, that you'd still wear them. But I noticed the way you looked at the flowers, your face falling. I promise I'll bring you a fresh garland tomorrow, but I'm still not sure how to keep them fresh on the bus ride home. I may have to learn some magic for that."

Priya giggled. "Thatha, that's so sweet! Did Paati wear the flowers even though they wilted?"

"Oh yes," Krishna replied with a fond smile. "Your Paati never cared about things being perfect. To her, the thought was enough."

Priya's face softened, and she fell silent, thinking about her grandmother in a new light. She hadn't known Radhika beyond the warm, gentle figure who had cooked her favourite sweets and told her stories at bedtime. She hadn't known this younger, more vibrant Radhika who had once been the centre of her grandfather's world.

"Thatha," Priya asked suddenly, "do you miss Paati?"

The question was simple, but it struck Krishna deeply. He took a moment to answer, his voice soft. "Every day, kanna. I miss her every single day."

As he spoke, Krishna felt the weight of all the letters he'd written over the years, each one a reminder of Radhika's constant presence. And though she was no longer beside him, her absence somehow felt like a presence of its own, filling his heart and his memories.

In the days that followed, the letters became a quiet ritual. Krishna found himself reading them to his family, one by one, each letter a piece of their shared history. Anita and Ravi would listen, sometimes with laughter, other times with misty eyes. They discovered stories they'd never heard before—small quarrels, days spent making do with little, unexpected joys that Radhika had infused into their lives.

One evening, as they sat around the dining table, Anita spoke up. "Appa, I always thought Amma was just...well, Amma. But hearing these letters, I feel as if I'm meeting a different person—a younger, more spirited version of her."

Krishna nodded, his eyes bright with pride. "Yes, that was your mother. She was always spirited. Even when times were hard, she had a way of laughing that made everything seem lighter."

Ravi, who had always been more reserved, looked thoughtful. "Appa, I remember her cooking for all of us during festival times. She would insist on making everything from scratch. I always thought she just loved cooking, but...now I think she did it to bring us all together."

Krishna smiled, knowing that Ravi was finally seeing the depth of his mother's love, expressed through her simple, everyday acts of care. Radhika had been the heart of their family, the steady warmth that had kept them connected, even when they hadn't noticed.

One evening, Krishna came across a particularly difficult letter to read. It was written shortly after their second child had been born, during a period when money was tight, and he was often too tired to talk much. The letter was a reflection of that time, filled with apologies for not being the husband he wanted to be, for being distant when Radhika needed him.

As he read it silently, the memories came flooding back—the sleepless nights, the endless bills, the quiet despair he had felt but never voiced. Radhika had understood, of course. She had been his pillar, lifting him up with her gentle reassurance. Even now, he felt a pang of guilt for the sacrifices she'd made, the quiet burdens she had carried without complaint.

Krishna took a deep breath, and decided not to read this one aloud. Some memories were too personal, too painful to share. Yet, as he sat there, Anita noticed the sombre look on his face and placed a comforting hand on his shoulder.

"It must have been difficult, Appa," she said gently. "But you both made it through. You and Amma gave us everything."

Krishna looked up at his daughter, seeing in her face the same resilience that had once been Radhika's. "Yes," he murmured. "Your mother gave us all more than I could ever repay. I only hope...I only hope she knew how much I loved her."

Anita's eyes filled with tears, and she squeezed his hand. "She did, Appa. We all knew."

Ravi, seated across the table, looked at his father with newfound respect. "You were both strong, Appa. All these letters...they're a reminder of everything you went through, and everything you built together."

Krishna's heart swelled, and he felt a strange, profound sense of gratitude—for his family, for the life he'd shared with Radhika, and for the chance to relive it all through these letters. They were a gift he hadn't realized he'd given himself, a way to keep Radhika's memory alive and to show his children that love was not just a feeling but a journey, a series of small acts that held them all together.

That night, as he tucked the letters back into their box, Krishna felt a deep peace settle over him. Radhika's love had been the foundation of their family, and now, through these letters, it would continue to live on, binding them even in her absence.

The box was returned to its place, but now, its presence felt less like a relic of the past and more like a bridge—connecting the memories of yesterday with the family of today. Krishna realized he didn't need the letters to remember Radhika, but somehow, knowing they were there made her feel just a little closer, as if she were still there, watching over them all.

In the weeks that followed, Krishna's life began to revolve around those letters. They became a quiet, almost sacred time each evening, as he would take one out, run his fingers over the faded ink, and read either in silence or aloud to his family. His children and grandchildren now looked forward to these gatherings, listening with a reverence that both comforted and surprised him. They were seeing a side of Radhika and of their own lives that had long been buried under the everyday routines and busyness of the world.

It was one such evening, in the dim warmth of his study, that Krishna discovered a letter that seemed different from the others. Its envelope was worn, edges frayed as if it had been handled more often, and inside, the words seemed hastily written, unlike his usual careful handwriting.

As he began reading, his heart stirred with the memory of the time this letter had been written. It was from one of the most challenging periods of their life together, a time when he and Radhika had faced a sorrow that had threatened to tear them apart.

"Dearest Radhika,

I don't know how to find the right words for this. I keep thinking that if I write it down, maybe I'll understand it better, or at least make sense of the silence between us. I'm sorry. I don't know how else to say it. I'm sorry for not being there for you, not in the way you needed. I see the pain in your eyes, and it kills me to know that I can't take it away.

Every time I look at you, I feel as though I'm losing you, piece by piece. I know you're hurting, and I wish I could fix it, but I don't know how. You once told me that all we had to do was hold on to each other, and everything would be alright. So, I'm holding on, Radhika, in the hope that maybe we can find our way back to each other. I love you, and I'm not going to let go."

Krishna's hand trembled as he finished reading. He remembered that time all too well—the loss they had faced, the grief that had settled into their lives like a heavy shadow. They had lost their firstborn, their son, to a sudden illness when he was barely three years old. The sorrow had been unimaginable, and he had felt helpless as he watched Radhika retreat into her own silence. It had been a long time before they could even speak about it, before they found a way to grieve together rather than alone.

The memory still stung, but as he sat there, he realized that it was another testament to their love, a reminder of how they had clung to each other even in the darkest of times. It was not a love built on grand gestures or words, but one woven from resilience and forgiveness, from the shared understanding that no pain could truly separate them.

That night, Krishna didn't share the letter with his family. Instead, he held it close to his heart, silently thanking Radhika for the strength she had given him, for the unspoken promise that had bound them together even when they had felt lost. This letter, he realized, was something he wanted to keep just between them, a memory to cherish in the quiet of his own heart.

The next day, as Krishna sat in his study, Anita walked in, her eyes thoughtful.

"Appa, I've been thinking," she said softly. "I'd like to keep these letters safe. Maybe we could bind them together—preserve them somehow, so that generations after us can know your story. Yours and Amma's."

Krishna felt a swell of emotion at her words. He looked at her, pride filling his heart. "You know, Radhika would have liked that. She was always telling me that stories were meant to be shared, passed down."

Anita nodded, her eyes misty. "Yes, and these letters are more than just memories. They're a part of our lives, of who we are."

As they talked, Ravi entered, joining the conversation with a gentle smile. "Appa, we want you to know that we understand now. We understand what you and Amma went through for us. I never thought much about your sacrifices, but these letters have taught me so much."

Krishna's heart filled with warmth as he looked at his children, finally seeing them understand the depth of the love that had sustained their family. The letters, he realized, had done more than just preserve memories—they had brought his family closer, bridging the gap between the past and present in a way he hadn't imagined possible.

Priya, who had been listening quietly from the doorway, spoke up. "Thatha, will you tell me more about Paati's favourite things? I want to know what she loved."

Krishna smiled, feeling Radhika's presence in the room. "Well, let's see," he began, a twinkle in his eye. "She loved jasmine flowers, as you know. And she loved music, especially old Carnatic songs. But more than anything, she loved all of you. She used to say that seeing her family together was her greatest joy."

As he spoke, he realized that Radhika's love had not faded with her absence—it had only grown, blossoming into the hearts of their children and grandchildren, living on through the simple, everyday moments that had once bound them.

A few weeks later, the family gathered for a small ceremony. They had taken Krishna's letters, carefully preserving them in a handmade book with the title Letters to Radhika etched on the cover. It was a modest binding, yet elegant, crafted with a love that echoed Radhika's own simple grace.

As they stood together, Ravi placed the book in Krishna's hands. "Appa, this is for you. And for Amma. A piece of both of you, for all of us."

Krishna's eyes filled with tears as he held the book, feeling the weight of the years and the love, they had shared. He opened the cover, tracing his fingers over the first letter he'd written all those years ago. The ink had faded, but the words were as clear in his heart as ever.

With his family gathered around him, he felt a sense of completion, a fulfilment of the promise he had once made to Radhika—that he would always hold on to her, no matter what life brought. In these letters, he had found a way to keep that promise, to let Radhika's love live on through the generations that would follow.

As they stood there, Krishna felt Radhika's presence once more, a gentle warmth that filled the room. He knew that she was watching, perhaps even smiling, knowing that her love had indeed endured, as timeless and steady as the turning of the seasons.

And as he closed the book, he knew that he had not only preserved their memories, but had also created a legacy—a testament to a love that was woven through the very fabric of their family, binding them together long after the letters had faded.

The Tea Seller's Wisdom

Moideen was an ordinary man by many standards, but in the small village of Perumannoor, he was something of a legend, or rather, a relic. He had once been the tea seller at a bustling railway station, right at the heart of the nearby town of Thriprayar. Though his life was simple, the station had offered him glimpses into the vast world that lay beyond his village, filling his years with endless stories of travellers, families, and strangers alike.

Now, he was a familiar figure on his verandah, leaning back on a creaky wooden chair, gazing into the distance with a faint smile, as though he were watching the trains pass by once more. His hair had turned to wisps of silver, and his thin frame had grown frail with age, but his eyes still sparkled with a mixture of wit and wisdom, hinting at the many memories he carried within him.

It was his grandson, little Imran, who brought a glimmer of activity to Moideen's slow-paced days. Imran, a seventeen-year-old with a knack for technology, had recently started a local blog. It was a humble affair, mostly read by the curious village folk and a few distant relatives, but it had given Imran a purpose and Moideen a new audience.

One rainy afternoon, Imran came to his grandfather with a proposition. He wanted to interview Moideen about his life at the railway station, the stories he'd gathered, and the lessons he'd learned. The boy had sensed that there was something timeless in Moideen's tales—a warmth, a wisdom—that could bring a fresh perspective to their community.

The old man looked at Imran thoughtfully, a glint of pride dancing in his eyes.

"So, you think the people here will want to read about an old tea seller?" he asked, with a hint of amusement.

"Of course, Acha," Imran said, using the affectionate term for grandfather. "People don't have time to listen to stories like they used to. But online... well, maybe they'll find time to read them."

Moideen chuckled, shaking his head. "Very well, let's see if the stories of an old man can still stir up something in this young world of yours."

And so, with the rain softly pattering on the tiled roof, Moideen began to tell his first story.

Moideen's tea stall had been a small, wooden kiosk by Platform Number Three, squeezed between a newspaper stand and an old banyan tree that seemed as ancient as time itself. From dawn till dusk, he had brewed countless cups of tea—spiced, sugary, and always piping hot. He served anyone who came along, from weary travellers to the bustling hawkers who would dart across the platform, selling everything from peanuts to trinkets.

"On some days," Moideen said, his voice drifting as if he were seeing it all again, "I felt like I knew every soul who passed through the station. But in truth, most of them were strangers. The faces would come and go, like waves at the shore, but a few... a few left a mark."

He paused, a smile teasing at his lips. "There was one man, a doctor from Thrissur. Every Thursday evening, he would come to catch the 6:15 train, a patient and thoughtful man. He'd sit on the bench in front of my stall, waiting, reading his newspapers."

Moideen's voice softened as he continued. "One evening, he ordered two teas. I asked him if someone would be joining him. He just looked up and said, 'Ah, no, Moideen. Today, I am remembering an old friend."

The doctor had smiled, but there was a sadness in his eyes that Moideen had learned to recognize. It was the look of someone who had loved and lost. He had handed him the teas and stepped back, watching as the doctor sipped from one cup, then the other, in quiet remembrance. It had been a silent ritual, one that the doctor repeated each week for many months.

"That doctor," Moideen said, shaking his head slowly, "taught me that even tea could be an offering, a way to honour the past."

As he spoke, Imran typed furiously, barely keeping up with his grandfather's words. He had never imagined his Acha's life could have been so rich, so filled with the quiet beauty of human connection. But there was something more, something in Moideen's voice that seemed to reach out, touching not only the mind but the heart as well.

"Wasn't it lonely, Acha? All those people, coming and going?"

Moideen's eyes crinkled with a smile. "Lonely? Perhaps, but I had my share of laughter too. There was a young soldier, not much older than you, who would come by once in a few months to catch the train home. He'd tell me his stories—about the drills, the hard life in the barracks—and he always said, 'One day, Moideen-ikka, I'll bring my family here, and they'll see how my Acha makes the best tea on this side of Kerala!'"

"But he never did?" Imran guessed, sensing the story's bittersweet turn.

"No, he didn't," Moideen replied, his voice quieter. "The war came, and he... he didn't return."

For a moment, there was only the sound of the rain outside, the gentle rhythm a fitting backdrop to the tender memories unfolding in Moideen's heart.

"People are like trains," he said finally. "They come and go, some stop longer, others pass in a flash. But if you're lucky, you'll find a few who make the journey worthwhile."

The next day, Imran published the story on his blog, calling it "The Wisdom of Platform Number Three." By evening, the post had attracted more attention than he had ever expected. Friends, neighbours, and even strangers left comments, sharing their own memories of long-forgotten station stops, their own encounters with tea sellers, or simply thanking Moideen for his words.

Moideen was touched, though he would never admit it. He had thought his stories were just that—his own memories, faded with time. But now, seeing the warmth with which people responded, he felt a strange, unexpected sense of belonging.

It wasn't long before Imran returned with a notebook and his old recorder, urging Moideen to continue. And so, day by day, Moideen spoke of the travellers he had met and the tales they had left behind, of fleeting friendships, sorrowful farewells, and, at times, the little miracles that seemed to happen only in the presence of tea and trains.

One afternoon, as Imran sat listening, Moideen recalled a story that had been dear to him for many years—a story of a little girl, perhaps six or seven, with big, curious eyes.

"She was alone, standing there on the platform, clutching a small cloth bag," Moideen began. "I remember it was a hot day, and she looked so lost. So, I went over and offered her a cup of water. When she took it, she asked, 'Uncle, where do the trains go when they leave here?'"

Moideen chuckled softly, his laughter like the rumble of an old train. "Ah, I didn't know what to tell her! I just said, 'They go to all the places you can dream of, little one.'"

The girl had looked at him with wonder, her eyes wide as if he had given her the key to some magical world. And perhaps, in a way, he had. For as she had waited for her parents to return, Moideen had told her tales of the places the trains went, of distant cities, misty mountains, and coastal towns where the sand sparkled like gold.

"She probably doesn't remember me," Moideen said, smiling, "but I like to think that I left her with something—an idea, a dream."

Imran listened intently, capturing every word, realizing that this was more than just a collection of stories. It was a testament to his grandfather's life, a life that was ordinary yet extraordinary in its quiet impact.

Soon, the village buzzed with talk of Moideen's stories. People would come by, waving to him from the gate, asking him about the latest tale, or simply thanking him for reminding them of life's small, precious moments.

Moideen found himself not only revived by the attention but reconnected with the world in a way he hadn't expected.

And as he continued to share his memories, he noticed a change in himself too. The days no longer felt so empty. He had become a storyteller, an elder with wisdom that people sought out, a reminder that every life—even the life of a humble tea seller—held within it an entire world of meaning.

Little by little, Moideen's presence on Imran's blog became something of a local treasure, a cherished corner of the internet where people gathered to reminisce, reflect, and remember the lessons life had taught them.

And in turn, Moideen found himself alive once more, his heart as full as his memories, as he continued to share the quiet wisdom of a life spent by the railway tracks.

As the sun dipped low on the horizon, casting its warm glow over the village, Moideen leaned back in his chair, gazing at the small crowd that had gathered outside his house. They were waiting for his next story, eager to hear from the man who had once been just a tea seller but had become something more—a bridge between the past and the present, a keeper of stories that would linger in their hearts.

Moideen smiled to himself, feeling the gentle satisfaction of a life well-lived, and perhaps, he thought, just a bit of the thrill he had once felt on the bustling platform of Thriprayar, with trains and tales forever passing through.

The stories continued, each day revealing another facet of Moideen's life. The railway station, with its ceaseless traffic of trains and travellers, had offered him more than just work; it had given him companionship, excitement, and an ever-changing cast of characters. To the people of Perumannoor, Moideen's stories brought laughter, sorrow, and a growing realization that even the simplest life could hold profound wisdom.

One afternoon, Imran arrived with his notebook, already anticipating a new story. But as he sat beside his grandfather on the verandah, he noticed a reflective, almost wistful expression on Moideen's face.

"What is it, Acha?" Imran asked, sensing something different.

Moideen leaned back, folding his hands across his lap. "I was just thinking of an old friend, someone who once showed me the importance of kindness."

Imran's interest was piqued. "Another traveller?"

"No, not a traveller," Moideen said with a smile. "A tea seller, just like me."

Moideen's tea stall, though small, had once stood as a cornerstone of Platform Number Three. But there was another stall, stationed just across the tracks on Platform Number Four, owned by a man named Shankaran. Shankaran was an older fellow, with a long white beard and a laugh as loud as a train whistle. Every morning, Moideen and Shankaran would nod at each other from across the railway tracks, exchanging a silent greeting that had become a ritual over the years.

They had little in common beyond their trade, but there was a quiet bond between them. The tea sellers' code, Moideen called it. Whenever he ran out of sugar or milk, Shankaran would send his young assistant scurrying over with supplies. In return, Moideen would offer Shankaran extra tea leaves or a handful of cardamom whenever he had more than he needed.

But one scorching afternoon, when the sun blazed mercilessly, something happened that Moideen would never forget. It was a quiet hour between trains, and the platform was nearly empty. Moideen was resting on his stool, fanning himself, when he saw Shankaran waving urgently from across the tracks.

Curious, Moideen hurried over, leaping down onto the tracks and climbing back up to Platform Number Four. Shankaran was panting, his face flushed, and he grasped Moideen's arm as soon as he arrived.

"Moideen," he said breathlessly, "I need your help."

Moideen, startled by the urgency in Shankaran's voice, nodded without hesitation. "Tell me, brother. What's happened?"

"There's a boy," Shankaran said, pointing towards the edge of the platform. Moideen looked over to see a thin, bedraggled boy, barely ten years old, curled up on a bench. His clothes were torn, and he looked exhausted, as though he hadn't eaten in days.

"He showed up this morning," Shankaran continued. "Doesn't speak much, but I think he's run away from somewhere."

Without a second thought, Moideen and Shankaran put their heads together, concocting a plan to help the boy. They pooled their earnings from the morning, gathering enough to buy him some bread, bananas, and a train ticket to the nearest shelter where the railway police could help him.

As they handed the boy the food, he looked at them with wide eyes, a flicker of hope replacing the emptiness in his gaze. The two men watched as the boy devoured the bread and fruit, his small face lighting up with gratitude. It was a simple act, a small kindness, but for Moideen, it was a memory that stayed with him.

"That boy taught me something, Imran," Moideen said softly. "Sometimes, we meet people for just a few moments, yet those moments leave a mark on our hearts."

Imran nodded, jotting down the story, his admiration for his grandfather growing with each word. He hadn't realized just how much wisdom his Acha held, nor how these seemingly ordinary stories carried messages that were timeless and profound.

The blog post featuring Shankaran and the boy struck a chord with readers, sparking discussions throughout the internet readers. Some spoke of their own encounters with strangers who had changed their lives; others thanked Moideen for reminding them of the importance of small acts of kindness. For Moideen, however, these responses were simply a reminder of the joys and sorrows he had witnessed over the years.

As Imran continued to chronicle Moideen's life, more visitors began to arrive at the house, eager to hear his stories firsthand. Neighbours, friends, and even a few curious strangers gathered on the verandah each evening, listening as Moideen shared tales from his days on the platform.

One evening, as a gentle breeze blew through the village, a man in his forties approached the verandah. He was dressed in a simple white shirt, his face lined with the traces of a life spent under the sun. He stood quietly, listening to Moideen recount a story, his gaze fixed intently on the old man.

After the story ended, the man stepped forward, clearing his throat.

"Moideen-ikka," he said, using the respectful term for elder, "do you remember me?"

Moideen squinted, studying the man's face. There was something familiar about him, a faint resemblance to someone he had once known, but he couldn't quite place it.

"I'm sorry, my friend," he replied, shaking his head. "My memory isn't as sharp as it used to be."

The man smiled, stepping closer. "I was the boy—the one you and Shankaranetan helped all those years ago."

A hush fell over the crowd, and Moideen's eyes widened as he stared at the man, his heart leaping with recognition. He reached out, his hand trembling, and the man took it, clasping it tightly.

"You saved me that day," the man said, his voice thick with emotion. "I don't know where I would have ended up if it hadn't been for your kindness."

Moideen felt a lump rise in his throat, a mixture of joy and disbelief filling his heart. He had thought of that boy often over the years, wondering what had become of him. To see him now, grown and standing before him, was nothing short of a miracle.

Imran watched in awe, realizing that this was more than just a story—it was a testament to his grandfather's legacy, a reminder of the impact that one person's kindness could have on another's life.

The man stayed for a while, sharing his journey with the group. He had found work, built a family, and now travelled around helping young people in need, inspired by the compassion Moideen and Shankaran had shown him. As he spoke, Moideen's eyes sparkled with pride, and he knew that Shankaran, wherever he was, would have been proud too.

In the days that followed, the story of the "lost boy" spread throughout Perumannoor. People began to see Moideen in a new light, not just as a retired tea seller, but as a man who had quietly shaped lives, one cup of tea at a time. Even the village elders, who rarely ventured out, started visiting Moideen, drawn by the wisdom he offered and the warmth he exuded.

One evening, as Moideen and Imran sat on the verandah, watching the sun dip below the horizon, Imran turned to his grandfather with a question that had been weighing on his mind.

"Acha," he began, hesitating. "Do you miss the railway station? All those years, all those people… doesn't it feel strange to be away from it all?"

Moideen looked out at the village, his gaze softening. "Yes, I miss it sometimes," he admitted. "There's a certain magic in the noise, in the rush of trains and the flow of people. But life is like the railway station, Imran. People come, and people go. And we each have our own platform, our own place in the journey."

He paused, placing a hand on his grandson's shoulder. "But you know what I don't miss? The feeling of loneliness. Because now, I have you, and I have these stories to share."

Imran felt a warmth spread through him, realizing that his project had become more than just a blog. It was a bridge between generations, a way to keep his grandfather's memories alive.

That night, as Imran published the latest post, he couldn't help but feel a deep sense of gratitude for his grandfather.

Moideen's stories had shown him that life's true richness lay in the connections we forge, the kindness we extend, and the wisdom we pass on.

And as he watched the comments pour in—each one a testament to the lives his grandfather had touched—Imran knew that Moideen's legacy would live on, not just in the words on the page, but in the hearts of everyone who read them.

The weeks passed, and Moideen's fame grew quietly but steadily. Villagers, who had once seen him as just an old tea seller, now came to his house, bringing their own stories, seeking his advice, or simply enjoying his tales of the bustling railway station. Imran, too, felt a sense of pride he hadn't known before; he had always admired his grandfather, but only now was he realizing how special Moideen's life truly was.

One day, as they sat on the verandah with a small crowd gathered around, Moideen began to tell a new story. This one was different, though; it was not about a train passenger or a fellow tea seller, but about himself.

"I was just sixteen when I took my first job," Moideen began, his voice soft but steady. "My family was poor, and I was the eldest. My father worked the fields, my mother kept the house, and it fell on me to find some way to earn."

The crowd listened with rapt attention, many of them surprised. They'd heard so many of Moideen's tales, yet rarely had he spoken about his early years.

"My first job," he continued, a hint of a smile on his lips, "was as a porter at the same station where I would later sell tea. The work was hard, hauling heavy luggage and crates, sweating in the hot sun and standing in the monsoon rains. But I was young, and there was a joy in the work, in feeling that I was helping my family."

Moideen looked at his hands, rough and calloused even after all these years. "It was there that I first met the people who would become my friends, my brothers. The other porters, the vendors, the coolies... we were all bonded by our work, by the shared understanding that each day brought a new struggle."

Imran, scribbling furiously, paused and looked up, captivated by the emotion in his grandfather's voice.

"One day," Moideen continued, his eyes misty, "an elderly man arrived at the station, alone and frail. He was carrying a bundle of clothes and a small brass box. I remember it well, because he could barely lift the box. I went over, took it from him, and walked him to his platform. He thanked me, and we began to talk as he waited for his train."

Moideen paused, as though lost in the memory. "The man told me he was going to visit his daughter, whom he hadn't seen in years. She had moved to the city, found work, and raised a family of her own. He spoke about her with such pride, but also with a hint of sadness. 'Children grow up, Moideen,' he told me, 'and they forget the hands that held them when they were small.'"

The crowd was silent, listening intently to each word. Imran, too, felt a weight in his heart, sensing that this story held a lesson deeper than the others.

"When the train arrived," Moideen continued, "the man held my hand tightly and said, 'Remember, people will come and go in life, but kindness will always stay with you. Be kind, Moideen. That is all that matters.'"

The old man's words had stayed with Moideen, shaping his life in ways he hadn't realized until now. For years, he had carried that simple philosophy in his heart, serving tea to strangers, lending a hand to those in need, and living a life defined by kindness.

Moideen looked up at the faces gathered before him, his eyes clear and bright. "That old man was right. Life is a railway station, and people are like passengers. They come and go, but the kindness we show each other stays forever. It's the only thing that really lasts."

Imran's blog post that night, titled The Kindness That Stays, was shared far and wide. People across the district read Moideen's words, moved by the simplicity and power of his message. Even the local newspaper picked up the story, featuring an article about the "Wisdom of Moideen, the Tea Seller of Perumannoor." The once-forgotten tea seller had become an unlikely hero, a symbol of the values that held communities together.

But Moideen, humble as ever, seemed unaware of his newfound fame. For him, it was enough to have Imran by his side, listening to his stories and giving them a place to live on. He hadn't sought recognition; he had simply lived his life, and now, in his twilight years, that life was finding new meaning.

One evening, as they sat together watching the fading light, Imran turned to his grandfather with a question that had been on his mind.

"Acha," he began, "why did you never tell us all this before? All these stories, all these memories… they're so precious."

Moideen chuckled, patting Imran's shoulder. "A story needs a listener, Imran. And I never had one—until you." He paused, gazing at the horizon. "I think every elder has stories to tell, wisdom to share. But sometimes, the world moves too fast, and we are left behind, like old stations along a forgotten route."

Imran felt a pang of guilt, realizing the truth in his grandfather's words. How many times had he brushed off Moideen's attempts to talk, too busy with his own life to listen?

"I'm sorry, Acha," he said, his voice low. "I should have listened sooner."

Moideen shook his head, a gentle smile on his face. "There is no right time, Imran. You came to listen when you were ready. And that is all that matters."

In the weeks that followed, Moideen's health began to decline. He grew frailer, his energy waning, yet he remained cheerful, his spirits lifted by the constant stream of visitors who came to hear his stories. Each person left with a smile, touched by the tea seller's wisdom.

One evening, as Moideen rested on his cot, he motioned for Imran to sit beside him. He reached under his pillow and pulled out an old, faded photograph. It was a picture of him as a young man, standing proudly at his tea stall with Shankaran by his side.

"Keep this," Moideen said, pressing the photo into Imran's hand. "It's a memory of who I was, of the life I lived. Someday, when you are old, perhaps you'll look at it and remember the stories I told you."

Imran held the photograph close, his heart heavy with love and sorrow. He could feel the weight of his grandfather's legacy, the wisdom and kindness that had defined Moideen's life.

"Thank you, Acha," he whispered, his voice choked with emotion.

Moideen smiled, his eyes gentle and wise. "Remember, Imran, life is short, like the time between trains. Be kind, be patient, and always listen. That's all I have to give you."

Moideen passed away quietly a few days later, leaving behind a legacy that would be cherished by everyone in Perumannoor. The village mourned him, not as a mere tea seller, but as a man who had taught them the beauty

of simple kindness. Imran, heartbroken but filled with pride, continued the blog in Moideen's memory, sharing his stories and wisdom with a growing audience.

The blog, now known as The Tea Seller's Wisdom, reached far beyond Perumannoor, touching hearts across the country. Readers found solace in Moideen's words, comforted by his gentle reminders of compassion and humility. Imran knew that his grandfather's spirit lived on, in each story and each lesson, a testament to a life well-lived.

And in quiet moments, when Imran sat alone, he would look at the faded photograph and remember the simple tea seller who had shown him the true meaning of life. He knew, deep in his heart, that he would carry Moideen's wisdom with him always, a beacon of kindness that would guide him, like a station light shining softly in the night.

Afterword

As I bring this collection to a close, I am reminded of the quiet power held by the stories we inherit and carry forward. In crafting these tales, I wanted to offer a glimpse into the lives of South India's elder generations—their joys, struggles, sacrifices, and legacies. These are not just individual stories; they are pieces of a larger, shared narrative, one that shapes us all in ways we may only understand with time.

Writing Wrinkleskin Stories has been a journey in honouring the richness of our roots. I hope these stories have offered you moments of connection and reflection. Perhaps you saw a glimpse of your own family members in these characters or felt the familiar warmth of a cherished memory.

In India, we have a saying that speaks to the importance of honouring one's elders, for they are the custodians of history and culture, bearers of wisdom, and guardians of tradition. Through these pages, I aimed to honour those who came before us and to remind us all of the strength and dignity that remain in lives lived fully. As you leave this book, I hope it has inspired you to listen to the elders in your own life, to share in their memories, and to keep their stories alive. They are, after all, our link to the past and a guiding light to our future.

Thank you for walking this path with me, and for sharing in the quiet beauty of these lives.

With gratitude,

Ashwin Kumar Iyer

www.ingramcontent.com/pod-product-compliance
Lightning Source LLC
LaVergne TN
LVHW041945070526
838199LV00051BA/2907